Survival

Of A

Queen

A novel by

Queen B.G.

ISBN : 978-0-9840077-4-5

LCN TBD

Interior Layout Design: Write On Promotions

Cover Layout Design: Cee Rider Graphics

Dedication

This book is dedicated to the men, women, and children that's living this street life. I may not know you but I feel you, I understand 100%, but it's more to life than this shit. Trust me, I use to be you....

Acknowledgements

I HAVE to thank God for the ability to do what I love to do, for where he's brought me from, and for where he's taking me. I am truly blessed.

A huge thank you to Justin Nichols, I really appreciate you for all the time and critiquing you gave me on this project. It truly means the world to me.

A big thank you to everyone that aided me in releasing another five star banger. Whether you proofread it, gave ideas/constructive criticism, or just gave me the extra motivation I needed to keep going I really appreciate you.

Of course I have to say thank you to my kids for being understanding and patient. Writing takes up a lot of time and sometimes I get so consumed in it that we miss an outing or two. But, they never complain and are always there showing their love. I love you *MUAH*

To my extended family; India, Cali Kim, Ni'cola Mitchell, Niccole Simmons, Sequaia Reed, Robert Womack, and the Cali Connect family, I appreciate all of you and I love you guys to pieces.

To my readers and supporters, I ABSOLUTELY LOVE YOU!!! It's your constant support that has gotten me this far and it's a constant reminder as to why I continue to do what I do. Words alone can't express how grateful I am to have people like you behind me 100%. Thank you, from the bottom of my heart.

To my biggest supporters: Chunky, Marissa Palmer, Sandy Barrett Sims, Gabrielle Dotson, and Carla Towns. Thanks ladies for your amazing support and feedback. You have showed me love since day one and I am forever grateful.

Finally, to the people out there who support me and has never had the opportunity to correspond with me. Thank you for your support. Regardless of how you heard about me or when, I appreciate the fact that you took a minute to experience my talent. I can only hope that you enjoy each and every experience that you have with me/my books and that you continue to support me throughout this journey. God Bless!

Survival

of a

Queen

Chapter One

"Help! Somebody help me please!" the young lady yelled frantically at whoever cared to listen at the time.

She moved swiftly but cautiously toward the young lady lying on the pavement just a few feet away from the curbside where a platinum colored IROC sat with the engine running. As she got closer to the unidentified woman, she noticed in her left hand was a single key with an alarm remote attached to it and in her right hand was a chrome .380 hand gun. The victim's purse lay spilled out beside her in the slowly growing pool of blood.

"Stay with me. You're gonna be okay, the ambulance is on its way. Just stay with me," she repeated while holding the victim's head in her lap.

Everything around them was in total chaos. Women and kids were screaming and trying their best to flee the scene. Men walked past looking through curious eyes, but never stopped to find out exactly what was going on. Shell casings covered the pavement as if they had replaced the raindrops that would normally fall during a slightly rainy day. While everything seemed to move in a very fast pace all around them, the woman holding the victim felt as if it was moving in slow motion. The ambulance was taking too long, no one had come to assist her with this woman, and because of her nervousness she heard her surroundings, but in a dragging type of way.

"Where are they?" she asked herself. "Baby just stay with me. You are gonna make it through this."

While stroking the victim's hair she felt as if she was helpless and needed to do something before this woman died right here in her arms. She looked down at her and began to pray a prayer that she hoped would change the outcome of this woman's life.

As she sat there, praying and rocking back and forth, the café owner kneeled down at her side and joined her in her prayer. There was a brief pause in her prayer as she looked at the man surprised but happy to have another prayer warrior at her side. As they continued their prayer, the victim lay bleeding, weak, and not making hardly any movement at all. One of the onlookers decided to approach, as well, to see if she could be of any assistance. When she did, she lost her mind, wishing the vision she had was simply a bad dream.

"No! No! No! Please god! No!" she said while breaking down at the sight of a familiar face. "KeKe get up. Come one baby, get up. What happened?" she questioned the store owner and woman that were previously at the victim's side.

"Two guys were shooting and when it was all said and done, she was lying here on the ground."

Looking down at her girl lying there on the pavement, NeNe noticed the car key and gun that were in her hands. She stuffed the gun in her purse and then ordered the woman to grab the rest of her things.

"Babe! Come help me," NeNe yelled while lifting KeKe from the ground. The panic in her voice alarmed him. When Sniper reached their presence his heart was broken by the sight of his little homegirl lying almost lifelessly in his girl's arms.

"Move! Move!" Sniper yelled while pushing everyone in arm's reach and scooping KeKe up as if she was a baby.

"Her car is right here," he said running toward her car. "I'm gonna take her to the hospital. Go get the truck and meet me there."

Sniper reached her car and noticed it was already running which gave him the impression that she must have been trying to get away.

"KeKe, Cuz, what the fuck? You gotta make it through this Cuz. You a fighter homegirl. I need you to just hang in there. I'm gonna have you at the hospital in no time," he said lying her down in the passenger seat.

As soon as he jumped in the car, he punched out using every bit of that 450 engine power to make it to the hospital as quickly as possible. Even as they left, there were no sirens heard or ambulance in sight. Had she laid waiting on them she would be dead for sure.

Sniper gangsta'd his way through every red light that he came to refusing to allow anymore dead time to pass that could ultimately cost him another one of his loved ones. And just as expected NeNe wasn't too far behind. The truck was parked just around the corner and there wasn't any traffic or a stoplight that was gonna stop her from catching up to them. While in route to the hospital NeNe managed to call a couple of homies to get the word out that KeKe was hit and headed to the hospital. Her final call, the most important call, was to Shawna.

"Hello."

"Shawna, this is NeNe. I'm calling you 'cause KeKe got shot and we're on our way to the hospital."

"Shot? What hospital?"

"Harbor UCLA."

With that said, the phone hung up and Shawna was on the first thing smoking to see what was going on. Her heart wasn't hurt, she wasn't angry, or anything. Her emotions were completely out of tune with what her brain was trying desperately to process but to no avail. There was no way in hell KeKe was down. That just wasn't an option. *KeKe is just too sharp for that*, she thought to herself. Even still, she traveled at high speeds to see if confirmation of what she had just heard would be given. It took about twenty minutes to reach the hospital and in that whole twenty minutes Shawna failed to shed a single tear.

ð∂ð

SKIRRRRRRRT!

The IROC came to a screeching halt right outside the emergency room doors. Sniper made his way to the passenger side of the car just as quick as his door had swung open and again he cradled KeKe in his arms and ran through the emergency doors yelling, "Help me! She's shot and she's barely breathing. Help!"

The nurse sitting at the desk came to his aid and ordered someone to bring a gurney. Just as they did, KeKe was gently placed on it leaving Sniper standing, covered in blood from the neck down.

"Get her to OR stat!" the nurse said in a loud, urgent tone.

Within seconds KeKe disappeared out of sight and NeNe came rushing through the sliding doors.

"Is she okay?"

Sniper didn't say anything. He just turned and punched the wall with a blow as powerful as one coming from Floyd Mayweather. On the drive to the hospital he talked continuously in an effort to keep KeKe alert. He figured if she just held on to his voice she had a chance at making it. Whether or not it worked was a different story. KeKe didn't move, didn't respond, cry, moan or anything. Other than the hope he carried in his heart, there was nothing to indicate that she was still alive. Now that she was in the hands of the doctors, Sniper feared the worst, but asked Allah to watch over her and grant her the ability to see another day.

In the operating room doctors and surgeons worked overtime, doing all that they could to prevent this from becoming another fatality. While examining their victim, they found that she was shot a total of six times. Her right forearm bore an entrance and exit wound verifying the bullet traveled through and through. Her left shoulder was also wounded just below her collar bone. The doctors referred to it as a flesh wound and continued to assess the victim. By this time an IV had been placed in her arm releasing fluids into her weak body. The doctor examining her found that two more shots had torn through her left leg shattering her tibia bone. Blood flowed freely from her head due to a minor graze to the head. Though the wound wasn't life threatening and hadn't caused any brain trauma, the gash the bullet left behind ran deep, exposing the white meat. Stitches were not enough to handle the job so the wound would be cleaned and repaired by placing a total of thirteen staples into her scalp. The most fatal wound of them all was a single gunshot wound to the chest that pierced through her lungs, causing them to collapse.

KeKe began convulsing rapidly and within seconds she stopped, displaying no movement at all.

Dr. Pultzier stated, "Let's hope that if internal bleeding is present, it's venous bleeding and not arterial bleeding."

The other surgeons working this case were in total agreement. If such a major artery had been ruptured, it would stop the oxygen flow from her heart to the rest of her body causing her to slip into a coma. After opening her chest cavity, he realized it was neither. Instead, it was capillary bleeding, which was confirmed by the slow oozing of blood. To make matters even worse, they discovered an infection was present and it needed to be treated as soon as possible.

While Dr. Pultzier worked to stop the bleeding, Dr. Tsani quickly inserted a breathing tube to aid KeKe in breathing since she could no longer do it on her own. Nurse Crenshaw administered a potion containing four different antibiotics through her IV to begin fighting off the infection. With all of the chaos going on in the operating room, the outcome was hard to determine. Just like Sniper, the surgeons remained hopeful and worked expeditiously to save the young woman's life.

ð̃ð̃ð̃

Meanwhile, in the waiting room, family and friends gathered in support of one another, exchanging heartfelt hugs and encouraging words. NeNe couldn't believe that this was happening. She always feared this day would come but never really believed in her heart that it would. When she looked up she came eye to eye with the most hurtful vision of all. Shell, KeKe's mom, was in tears pacing back and forth across the lobby floor. Her screams of hurt and pain echoed throughout the building as if she stood on a mountain top.

"Fuck that shit Cuz!" she yelled to the top of her lungs. "Why is my muthafuckin' baby in there fighting for her life and you muthafuckas sitting here like it's cool? Huh?"

No one responded because they knew this was her way of dealing with what was unraveling right before her eyes.

"Y'all don't hear me Cuz?" she asked upset that no one made a move or attempted to challenge her choice of words.

"Aye, what's up?" a voice stated right on cue. Everyone in the lobby turned to face the person with the familiar voice and

7

knew that this shit had just gotten real. Big Rocco, Ridah, Loc and Pookie walked through the sliding doors in unison displaying fiery eyes and that cold gangsta stride that only a true O.G. could hold.

"How is she doing?" Pookie asked while hugging his wife in an attempt to comfort her.

She remained silent, unable to speak due to the lump in her throat which seemed to be getting larger by the second. Because of her silence, NeNe stepped in to inform him of his daughter's status.

"She's still in surgery, so we're not really sure. They say she'll be in there for a while but when she came in, it wasn't looking good at all."

Having to tell him that was the worst feeling ever and it seemed to have affected everyone in attendance. Loc's head dropped toward the floor and Ridah leaned against the wall in a forward position allowing his head to do the same. Big Rocco shook his head in disappointment, feeling like he was at fault for allowing her life to run this crazy course. Sure, she was gonna make the choices she wanted to on her own, but he knew the influence he had over her. Instead of being stern about his feelings, he laid them by the wayside allowing her to make the very same mistakes he made at her age. For that, his heart was heavy and he concluded that he would never, ever forgive himself.

The waiting room began overcrowding as more and more people gathered to face an unpredictable outcome. The tension in the room was so thick you could cut it with a knife. A security guard entered the room requesting the visitors proceed to the waiting room just down the hall to avoid a fire hazard from happening. No one cared to acknowledge his orders, at least not anyone there on KeKe's behalf. They refused to separate just because some rent-a-cop said so. Family members of other patients began quickly giving up their chairs to avoid any problems resulting from this hostile crowd of individuals. While some people plotted on their next move and drove themselves crazy thinking the worst, Shawna sat silently in her seat unmoved and completely out of tune with her surroundings. This was her right hand girl and as far as she was concerned, KeKe was gonna walk out of there just as well as she was the last moment they had spoken. In her heart she knew that KeKe was gonna be just fine. She started to listen to some music on her iPod but her phone began ringing, displaying an unavailable number. Usually she would have ignored the call but her first mind said to answer it and she did.

"Hello?"

"This is Global Tel Link. You have a collect call from, Kai, an inmate in the Los Angeles County Jail System. To hear the maximum cost of this call, dial 4 now. If you would like to accept this prepaid call, dial 0 now. To block all future calls from this inmate please dial 5 now." Listening to this automated system had forced her to face the reality of what was happening. For the first time since she had gotten the disturbing call, Shawna accepted that everything was not alright and had to think fast in order to answer her cousin's call. The look in her eyes verified something was wrong and NeNe approached her to question what it was.

"What's wrong Shawna?" she asked in a whisper.

9

With that same whisper Shawna replied, "Kai is on the phone. What am I supposed to tell her?"

They both looked at each other in silence undecided on what to do, but still the call had to get accepted. After pressing 0 on the keypad, Shawna spoke into the phone just as calm as she would any other day.

"Hello."

"What's up cuzo? How's everything goin' out there?"

"Shhh," Shawna sighed. "Same crazy shit just a different day."

And she wasn't lying. This was the closest to the truth that she could have gotten without spilling the beans and she had absolutely no intentions on lying to her cousin at all.

"Yeah I feel ya. Have you talked to KeKe's crazy ass? I tried to call her but she didn't answer the phone."

Shawna didn't know what to say. Kai's question couldn't have come at a worse time. Out of everything in the world that she could have asked she chose this. *Are you fuckin' serious right now,* Shawna thought to herself. Now the battle was on. Being that Kai was in jail there was no way she was gonna tell her that KeKe was fighting for her life. It would send her on a cold spree that would not only result in a lot of people getting hurt, but in her facing more time and sitting in the hole unable to communicate with her loved ones. At the same time, they definitely didn't want her to find out from somebody else because that would be worse. Truth be told, shit traveled through the jail quicker than it ever did on the streets so it was only a matter of time that she found out.

"Hello?" Kai said wondering if Shawna heard her question.

"My bad, hold on one second okay?"

Shawna rose from her chair and began walking out the door to a much quieter place. If she was gonna do this, it was gonna be where she could talk to her in peace without the risk of someone spazzing out or having an emotional breakdown. Loc decided to accompany her outside to not only lend his support but to talk to Kai as well. Being that he was the closest person to KeKe, he knew without a doubt that he could convince Kai that he was gonna handle things. In every bad situation that has ever arisen in their lives, Loc was always their comforter and safety net.

"Kai, you there?"

"Yeah I'm here," she said still unaware of something being wrong.

"So how are you doing?"

"I'm cool, just ready to get up outta here. Did you hear me ask you about KeKe?"

Shawna looked at Loc, took a deep breath, closed her eyes, and let it out. "Kai," her voice was now soft and full of uncertainty, "I have something to tell you. You can't go wildin' out and stuff because we need you with a stable mind to help get through this."

11

Kai interrupted her speech, "Shawna, what the hell are you talking about? Is something wrong wit' my sister or...."

"Kai, KeKe is in the hospital."

"But she's okay right?" Kai asked afraid of what the answer may be.

"We don't know anything yet. She's still in surgery right now but as soon as we know something we'll make sure you know. You can call back whenever you want and I'll be sure to answer the phone."

Shawna hoped that the information she was giving was enough because she was afraid of what Kai's reaction might be once she told her the specifics.

"KeKe is a fighter. It ain't nothing her crazy ass can't pull through. What happened to her anyway? Don't tell me she found out she was pregnant again and been out there fightin' them raggedy hoes," Kai joked laughing into the phone.

"Naw, she's not pregnant." Shawna replied sadly.

"Well, what's wrong with her?"

"She got shot while she was over there by the café."

"And she at the hospital? Why she didn't just go to ole girl," and then it hit her. "Oh my god! Talk to me cuzo and tell me the truth. Is my sister fucked up man? Fuck this runaround you are giving me. Tell me what it is and let me deal with it."

12

Fuck, Shawna mouthed while looking to the ground placing one hand over her forehead unable to believe she was about to tell her this.

"She got shot I don't know how many times and from the way things were looking when she came in here, it's all bad."

Kai began screaming and Shawna could hear the phone receiver being beaten against the wall repeatedly.

"Noooooo! No! Fuck! Sh....," she heard through the receiver.

Tears formed in her eyes as she imagined how her cousin must feel going through this situation alone and under these circumstances. Loc interjected, grabbing the phone only to hear the same rage Shawna just witnessed seconds ago.

Fuck, he said to himself just as Shawna had when the unthinkable happened.

"Kai." There was no answer. "Kai?" he repeated softly trying to get her to calm down and acknowledge his presence.

Unfortunately Kai hadn't heard a thing and continued to go crazy on the phone. Loc could hear someone in Kai's background trying to calm her down but surprisingly not, Kai went on one. The conversation couldn't be heard clearly at this point but from what Loc was able to hear Kai was cursing that person out and threatened to kill them if they didn't back away from her.

"Kai!" he repeated, this time yelling with a voice full of authority.

Kai responded with that same authority but blended together with anger, "What!?!"

"Calm down Cuz. I know this shit is fucked up sis, but she gone be alright. When they let us in there to see her I need you to still be able to holla at her and let her know you here. You keep doin' that shit you doin' them punk ass deputies in there gone throw yo ass in the hole and it's gone be all she wrote. Listen to what I'm tellin you my nigga."

Kai continued to cry, but listened to him just as he knew she would. Their conversation continued on for a cool little minute and though the cries and the heartache never ended, their consoling words helped the both of them cope with what was going on. Kai decided she was ready to end the call, but not before making Loc promise he would make this right.

"Loc," she spoke softly in between sobs, "fix this! Promise me you are gonna fix this."

By that, he knew exactly what she meant and made that promise with no hesitation, "I promise sis, don't I always? This is what I do."

With that said, Kai was satisfied. They exchanged some "I love you's" and hung up the phone with the agreement that she would call back in a couple of hours to see what's up.

In the Twin Towers

Chapter Two

"OMG I can't believe this shit," Kai said with her hands on her head leaning against the wall next to the telephone booth.

After dropping her hands and leaning forward she placed her hands on her knees in a squatting position and asked God to please reverse this. While walking back to her cell, people that she associated with during her time in jail began asking questions as to what was wrong. No one got an answer, just pure silence as she moped down the tier like she had just lost her best friend. A couple of them wanted to press the issue in concern for their new friend, but knew from previous altercations that that would be a bad idea. Instead they let her be and hoped that she felt better, soon.

When she reached her cell she plopped down on her bunk and stared at the metal railing above, trying to grasp all that just happened. Her sister was all she had and now she was in jeopardy of losing her. And what would happen to Mai? Shit, what would happen to Harmony for that matter? Since she had been in jail, KeKe was the one providing for her daughter, financially. Bo was playing his position as a father, but financially he was unable to handle all that came with taking care of a child and still hold down the household and all of the extra bills Kai had acquired while out on the streets. Kai became stressed almost immediately. This was way too much to deal with and to top it all off, she had to appear in court in a couple of weeks. Speaking of court, she also made a mental note to holla at the detectives that were over her case. With this going on, everything about her case would have to change.

Just an hour after the phone call and lying on her bunk Kai began to feel sleepy. All of the tears she shed had caused her to lose her energy. She couldn't keep her eyes open to save her life. Though she fought long and hard, she went out like a light. She had literally cried herself to sleep.

ð ð ð

Bloom! Blam! Bam! Boom!

All of the noise from things falling in various directions, scattered across the counter top and falling on the floor startled Kai waking her up from her sleep. "What the fuck?" Kai said jumping up from the bottom bunk to find her celli picking up all of the contents that were knocked over.

"My bad, I didn't try to wake you up."

"What were you doing over there by my stuff anyway?" she asked.

16

"I was just gonna use some of your jalapeños for this spread."

This caused Kai to become furious. Before any other words were exchanged Kai was on her like a wolf in the wilderness. The poor lady couldn't understand how she had come to fight the only person she had ever befriended during their time of incarceration, but it was happening. Because Kai was much smaller than her, she was able to restrain her and question what she was thinking about. Had she been anyone else she would have fucked Kai up but she knew that something had to be wrong. This was totally out of Kai's character.

Their next door neighbor stood at the cells entrance and broke the news to Kai's cellie.

"Rumor has it her sister got popped and she not doin' too good."

That alone confirmed Kai's outburst and the woman helped Kai off the ground telling her, "I'm sorry about your sister man, but you can't just be flippin' out like that. That shit ain't cool. I'm too old to play games wit' yo young ass but I will put my foot off in yo ass if I have to."

Kai began crying frantically and knew that her cellie meant what she was saying and had her best interest at heart.

She was like a big sister to most of the inmates in the facility. She was twice their age, twice their size, and doing twice the amount of years they had been in this world. The only reason she was in the same facility as them was because of the new breakthrough of DNA analysis. She was now fighting another murder charge and was forced to be housed in the

17

County Jail instead of the State Prison where she'd resided the past twelve years of her life. Kai, just like many others, appreciated the balance provided by their fellow inmate. Her tears still flowed freely just as the throbbing in her heart continued. For the moment, it was something she had to hold deep inside. It was her only option if she wanted to follow the progress of her sister's health. Part of her felt bad, but for different reasons and it seemed to be too late to change what had already been done. Not only did she have to deal with the fact that her sister was seriously injured, but her conscious also. But what could she possibly do to fix what she had done?

Enough of all of this, Kai thought to herself while jumping up from her bunk. "I'm about to go call and check on my sister."

Looking ahead of her, Kai felt as if the tier had gotten longer. She walked down the long path preparing to face the music that, for a moment, had been placed on pause. The journey to the phone was never ending and the closer she came to that long awaited phone call, the more changes she experienced. Her throat felt as if it was closing up, butterflies fluttered rapidly in her stomach, sweat beads formed across her forehead, and her legs weakened due to the heavy lifting of her feet which felt like boulders of concrete. Even her hands were sweating. When she reached the phone, her body had frozen. Everything around her had stopped and became mute. For minutes, she stood there in a trance that seemed would never be broken. Then suddenly, her right arm stretched out in slow motion in an effort to grab the receiver. The number was dialed, the recording had started, and the moment of truth was near.

"Hello?" a voice said on the other end of the phone.

The recording started followed by the push of a button indicating the call was accepted, Shawna began speaking and within seconds Kai fell effortlessly to the floor landing with a loud thump.

Back At Harbor UCLA Medical Center...

Chapter Three

"This shit is takin' forever. They need to come tell us something, damn," Ridah said becoming more and more irritated as the time went by.

KeKe had been in surgery for almost four hours now and the anticipation was a bit overwhelming for everyone. While most of KeKe's family and friends still occupied the waiting room, NeNe and Sniper went back to the café where it happened to try and get some answers as to what happened. They had been gone for hours and Shawna couldn't wait until they returned with the news. Just as she was about to pick up the phone to dial NeNe's number, a tall, Asian man wearing a pair of light blue scrubs and a white lab coat entered the visiting room.

"Is the family of Keshawn Flower's here?" he asked unaware that the whole visiting room was there for her.

Everyone gave him their undivided attention and moved in closer toward him to be sure they heard him clearly.

"I'm her mother and this is her father," Shell said pointing from herself to her husband. "Is my baby okay? Can we go in to see her?"

"If you don't mind, I'd like to speak with the two of you privately?"

"Yeah we do mind. This right here," she said turning around stretching her arm out, pointing to all of the others that were in attendance, "is all a part of her family. We all deserve to hear what you have to say."

The doctor looked at her with uncertainty, but did as requested. "My name is Dr. Pultzier," he started accompanied by a firm handshake. "Your daughter was shot six times in various parts of her body. Once we began the surgery we discovered some internal bleeding. It took us some time, but we got the bleeding under control but not before it damaged the functionality of her organs. I'm sorry to have to inform you of this, but your daughter is in a coma and has been placed on life support."

The whole family went crazy. Shell collapsed in the arms of her husband and Shawna fell out of the chair onto the floor screaming, begging God to fix this, even if it's only this one time. The doctor stood in the midst of all of the chaos, waiting to answer any questions the parents may have.

"Can we see our baby Cuz," Pookie asked not really caring that he was addressing the doctor in a disrespectful manner.

"Sure. She's being set up in our ICU ward. You'll be able to go in shortly. Again, I'm sorry to have to inform you of this. If you have any questions feel free to call me."

With those words he gave Shell his card and turned to walk away. Big Rocco, being the most respectful of them all, stopped the doctor in his tracks, extended his hand to the doctor for a handshake and said, "Thank you."

The doctor returned the gesture, gave him his business card and made way back through the emergency room doors. About twenty minutes later, KeKe was clear to have visitors. Pookie and Shell went in first. While preparing to walk into their daughter's room the nurse said, "Excuse me. Because of the nature of this crime and her condition, we're gonna need you to establish a visiting list for the patient. Any and all persons not included on that list will be unable to see her."

"I'm not worried about no muthafuckin' list. My baby in here on a goddamn breathin' machine," Pookie said just as ignorant as he had always been.

"I understand, but unless you fill it out we can't accommodate your friends and family. Visiting will be limited to the two of you."

When put that way Pookie accepted the responsibility of providing a visiting list. There was no way he was gonna leave all the people that loved her out there in that waiting room without a chance to see her for what may be the last time. Although his reaction was unappreciated the nurse overlooked it as required by her job, and gave him a pen and paper. "Just bring it back to the nurse's station when you're done."

Pookie took the contents from her hand and entered the room. Both he and his wife began sobbing more than ever before. KeKe sat propped up on the bed with bandages on one side of her head, one leg wrapped in a thick layer of bandages with metal rods going through from one side to the other, a breathing tube traveled down her throat and was taped to her face to assist it in staying in the proper position, and scrapes and bruises scattered over her body from sliding on the ground. She lay still. Other than the diaphragmatic breathing, she made no movement at all.

"Look at you," Shell began yelling at KeKe as if she could hear what she was saying, "You always the one doin' some shit you ain't got no business doin'. What was it this time huh? Now look. You in here half dead not worried about how the fuck we feelin' right now."

The one way conversation went on and on and she continued to ask questions as if she was sure to get an answer. She blamed KeKe for her hurt, for all of the different emotions she experienced at the moment. Although she didn't mean it, it was easier to do than to accept the fact that she was losing her baby; her eldest child. The same child she gave up, the same child she had done wrong for quite some time, and most importantly the child that held everything together when she failed to do so. KeKe was stronger than she'd ever been, which made it even harder for Shell to accept the fact that KeKe couldn't make it through this. Even to her parents she had become somewhat invincible. Life, however, showed them differently. Once they released all of their messages to their daughter, they kissed her cheeks, said, "I love you" and walked towards the door hand in hand to allow the next visitor to come in. Just as they approached the nurse's station, the nurse stood to her feet preparing to ask for the visiting list. Before she could say a word, Pookie handed her the list and tried desperately to stop the tears that were building in the wells of his eyes.

Next to enter the room was Shawna and Loc. The two of them made way to her room totally unprepared for what lied before them. The mere sight of KeKe in this condition caused Shawna to pass out. Loc caught her just in time to break her fall and the nurses ran over to her aid. While they carried Shawna to the nearest wheelchair Loc decided to go ahead with his visit. This was his loc lying here in this bed. The only sister he'd ever had; the one person in the world that he trusted and loved wholeheartedly. When he reached her bedside he held her hand firmly in his and sat in silence trying to take it all in. The auburn colored chair with oak wood arms and legs was now pulled as close as it possibly could be to the hospital bed. Loc let the bed rail down to get a better view of her. Tears began rolling down his face as he released the most heart-filled words he could find at the moment.

"KeKe," there was a long pause before he cleared his throat and continued. "Man this shit is unbelievable to me. I really wish I could switch places with you right now because I would do it in a heartbeat. I don't know if you can hear me Cuz but I love you. You showed me what love was and how a person can really be your family and not share any blood at all. You are closer to me than anybody has ever been and I can't imagine losing you like this. I wish I knew who did this to you man. To tell the truth I really wish I coulda been there. I was supposed to protect you from shit like this. We did so much dirt together it was bound to come back on a nigga. But you? Naw, not you. I ain't even acceptin' that. You been through so much Cuz I feel like you deserve another chance; a better chance at life period. You are the strongest person I know so I know you can pull through this. Don't leave me KeKe Cuz. Fight this shit the same way you fight everything else. Do it for me. I need you Cuz. Mai need you. I mean, I got her my nigga just like I always do. As long as I got breath I'm gone make sure she straight but I can't do what you can do. Real talk can't nobody fill yo shoes. You gotta make it outta this you hear me? You have to. And I'm gone be here every day 'till you do. I can't do no mo' funerals; especially not yours. So take how long you need to take but yo ass better wake the fuck up one day. I love you Cuz on Crip, Foe death doe."

After those words he kissed her forehead and exited the room to go handle this business.

Chapter Four

"This shit is crazy. I can't wait till Loc get his ass over here so we can handle this business," Sniper said to NeNe while grabbing his black Pro 5 hoodie and his guns, headed down the hallway to the living room.

NeNe cried silently, really dying on the inside. It was situations like this that reminded her why she left the game in the first place. Her little home girl was on life support and now the only person in the world that loved her was about to go act a fool in the streets. Although she understood that this is how shit had to go, she feared losing her husband to this reckless lifestyle. All of the, "what if's" began flowing through her brain and caused her to feel a certain type of way. The only thing she could do at this point was hug and kiss her nigga and pray to God he has mercy on him.

Beep Beep Beep.

A car honked outside signaling that they were there. When NeNe looked out the window, Loc was in the driveway in a car that she'd never seen before. When she opened the door, Loc was approaching the stairs dressed in all black with a blue rag tied around his neck.

"Hey Loc," she said giving him a hug as he entered the door.

"Hey NeNe," he said in return.

"What's up Loc, Cuz?"

"You know what it is. I just left from the hospital and she still ain't budgin'. I'm hurtin' Cuz. They hit us where it hurt wit' this one."

"I know. But we bout to make sure they feel this shit homie," Sniper said with anger and tears building in his eyelids. His words matched his body language and it pierced NeNe's soul.

"So where we headed?"

"When NeNe talked to the business owners by the café they said it was two black dudes and they come there all the time. They think KeKe knew them because they are almost positive that she hugged one of them when she came. So that means we need to start knockin' on doe's to see what the streets are saying. Whoever did this is thinkin' they handled their business and it's only a matter of time before they slip up. In the meantime, we gone' go make some noise in these here streets to let niggas know we lookin'."

"Let's move then."

With those words, the two of them walked out of the door and hopped into the car. This wasn't your average low key vehicle either. The inside was flawless. Leather seats, fresh carpet, a cool sound system, and an in-dash TV were throughout. The interior's aroma was a mixture of cherries and cinna-berry that hung from the rearview mirror. Once the engine started Sniper let the seat back and began wiping down the gun and its bullets preparing to go to war.

ð ð ð

Almost an hour had passed and not one bullet was fired from their guns. Not one enemy revealed themselves on this cold, but sunny afternoon. It was as if the devil himself had sent out a warning that his soldiers were coming to snatch some souls. Unfortunately, it didn't change their plans nor their mindset. They were in killing mode and refused to go home without claiming the life of someone who would ultimately come hunt them down the same way.

"Let's stop by the café and see what they talkin' about up there."

"Cool," Loc replied while hopping in the turning lane to enter the freeway.

The two of them kicked back while Loc dipped through traffic listening to a mixed cd that was previously placed in the CD player. Ice Cube and Yo Yo were rockin' the mic with the infamous Bonnie and Clyde song. Soon as YoYo began spittin' her part, Loc lost it. This song was him and KeKe all day and it struck an even bigger nerve to have to listen to it knowing that his Bonnie was laid up in a hospital bed on a verge of going home to be with all the real gangstas that preceded her in death.

I'm the type of girl that rides for my nigga, I'll die for my nigga, peel a cap for my nigga.....

"Damn! We gotta find these bitch ass niggas homie for real. The song continued to add fuel to the fire which was already ignited and burning rapidly through the pit of his soul. The only way to put it out was the adrenaline and satisfaction that came with the release of hot lead into the body of the person that caused this pain in the first place. If it didn't happen fast, he was gonna explode.

Minutes later they had reached their destination. When Sniper exited the car, Loc did so also only he didn't go far. He simply leaned against the car, firing up a blunt filled with purple Kush while he scanned his surroundings looking for anything or anyone that was suspicious. Nothing seemed out of the ordinary so he continued to inhale the marijuana and relaxed against the passenger side of the car watching his homeboy enter the café.

"Hey man. How's it going?" Loc asked the café owner followed by a handshake and a shoulder to shoulder hug.

"I'm good man. What can I do for you today?"

"Well, I wanted to stop by and see if you had any new information for me. Anything would be helpful at this point man."

"I understand. Well like I told you before, the cameras were running but nothing was being recorded that afternoon for whatever reason. But…" the café owner said tapping Sniper on the shoulder signaling for him to follow him to the front door.

They stopped near the window of the café that was just before the front door and continued their talk with a clear view of the courtyard which was occupied by various types of people. Some enjoyed the newspaper, while others worked on their laptops or indulged in a conversation with one of their acquaintances.

"Do you see that brotha over there with the red polo shirt on, reading that magazine?"

Sniper glanced over at the man, "Yeah, what about him?"

"He was with the guy I saw hugging your sister that day. Maybe he can tell you something."

"Good looking out. I appreciate you man for real," he gave him a handshake and left out of the café headed towards the car where Loc stood waiting patiently.

His face bore a smile that sent a message that something good had come out of this and Loc was eager to find out what it was.

"What's up Cuz?"

"Aye, you remember I told you they said somethin' about KeKe huggin' a nigga right before that shit happened?"

"Yeah. Why?"

"You see that fool in the far right corner of the courtyard with that red polo shirt on?"

Loc began scanning the courtyard until he came across the guy Sniper was referring to, "Bingo!"

"The owner said that's the nigga who was with the dude that hugged her."

"Okay, so let's go merk this fool then."

Loc had already begun walking in the man's direction but was quickly stopped by Sniper's strong hold on his arm.

"What Cuz?"

Loc was getting hot. This was the moment they were waiting for and just like KeKe got knocked down in this courtyard, this nigga was fixing to do the same as far as Loc was concerned.

"Don't be stupid! Just like they just pointed him out to us, they will point yo ass out too. And, we need Cuz to take us to the other nigga. Let's just kick back and follow the nigga and see where he takes us."

Loc agreed and decided to fall back. Something better happen fast though because his trigger finger was itching and it was nothing like downin' this bitch nigga to help sooth it. Minute after minute, Loc became more and more impatient. His pacing back and forth was beginning to drive Sniper insane.

"Cuz, won't you sit your crazy ass down somewhere. You're beginning to make me nervous shit and that mean mug ain't helpin' the situation none either."

"Fuck that! I ought to go knock this niggas head off just on G.P. he sittin there smiling and shit like everythang is just smooth sailin' foe his ass and my home girl laid up in a hospital bed."

The more he talked, the more frustrated he became. Sniper sensed the sudden increase of anger and tried to defuse the situation before it worsened any further.

"Let's bend a corner real quick."

Loc gave no response. Instead, he stood with his head slightly lowered and his eyes squinted, focusing on his prey. His body began rocking from side to side in a slow pace while his hands caressed one another as if temptation stood directly in front of him anxiously awaiting his touch. Sniper knew this was bad. Everything in him said so. And just when he was about to try his tactics one last time Loc snapped.

"Man…. Fuck this!"

"Loc!" He didn't answer. Nor did he stop his movement. "Loc!"

Still it did nothing to prevent him from fulfilling his mission.

"Aw shit," Sniper whispered knowing his best bet was to follow Loc's lead because shit was about to get real. As soon as Loc reached the table where Miles sat completely unprepared for what was to come, shit hit the fan.

"Aye homie, get yo bitch ass up," Loc demanded using his hands to get his point across and moving the chair out of his way.

Miles stood to his feet, not because he was told to, but to check this nigga for thinkin' he was callin' some kind of shots. "Who the fu….."

Before he could even think about finishing his statement Loc swung on him knocking him completely over the table and onto the pavement.

"Cuz, get yo weak ass up," Loc said subduing him at the same time. Miles hurried to his feet and tried throwing a right hook that would never connect with its intended target. Unfortunately for him, he wasn't so lucky. Loc released punch after punch hammer after hammer on his ass and all of them connected sending an excruciating pain shooting through his body. Seeing that he was no match for Loc, Miles did the one thing he knew he could do to get this big ass nigga up off of him. He reached for his .9mm and attempted to send Loc home to meet his Maker. Little did he know, Loc wasn't alone. Sniper noticed the gun that sat snuggly in his waist line and kicked him directly in his ass sending him crashing down to the pavement once again.

"Naw Cuz, I got this. Let me beat this niggas ass."

Loc was upset that Sniper intervened at first because he wanted to demolish his sorry ass the way he knew he could. It wasn't until Miles had hit the pavement the second time that Loc noticed the gun in his possession and went stone retarded on his ass.

"Bitch! Yo hoe ass was gone try to shoot me Cuz," Loc asked while standing over him literally beating his ass to a pulp.

The onlookers watched in disbelief as the guy they were used to seeing act like a tough guy got his ass beat. Pleased with the damage that he'd done, Loc stopped his violent outburst and decided to fulfill his promise to his homegirls and Mai. The same gun that Miles intended to use in his defense was snatched up, cocked, and placed against his forehead. The look in Loc's eyes was like nothing Sniper had ever seen before. His homeboy was really about to do this. Right here, right now. A devilish grin spread across his face as he looked his enemy in his eyes and squeezed the trigger.

POW!

Was all you heard before the crowd began to run releasing screams of fear that could be heard down the block.

"What the fuck!" Loc yelled after Sniper grabbed his arm and held it to the sky.

"What I tell you cuz? Let's go before we catch a muthafuckin' case out here," Sniper said.

Just as quick as he had grabbed Loc's hand, Miles got up from the ground and took off runnin'. Loc and Sniper did the same and hopped in the car and sped away.

"Cuz, what the fuck was you thinkin' about?" Loc asked ready to knock the shit outta Sniper. "You almost made me wanna shoot yo ass with that bullshit you just pulled. Why you didn't let me shoot the nigga?"

"What was I thinkin'? Fool I was thinkin' about that life sentence you was about to get our ass. I told yo ass before you did that shit that we needed this nigga to take us to his partna. Stop actin' off of emotions homie and be smart. Besides, that ass whoopin is gonna send a message to whoever else played a part in this shit."

As much as Loc hated to admit it, Sniper was right. But damn, it sho felt good to have KeKe's attacker at the other end of the barrel. The thought of it put a smile on his face and he was gonna love telling his homegirl how he had dogged his ass, when he goes to the hospital to visit her tomorrow.

Pitcheous Detention Center

Chapter Five

In the day room everyone was spread throughout doing whatever it was that occupied their time for the moment. Some played cards while others either watched television or engaged in humorous conversations. Amongst those occupying the dayroom was KeKe's baby daddy, TG. He had been brought back down on a new case and placed in the county jail. Chit chatting with these lame ass niggas wasn't even an interest of his. All he wanted to do was watch a little TV before it was time to lock it down. He smiled to himself as the Sunburst commercial aired because he could picture KeKe's ass poppin' it just like that, singing, *"drop it like it's hot... drop it like it's hot."*

Just as quick as that smile had spread across his face, it disappeared. Channel 9 News displayed some breaking news that caused his heart to crumble.

"We're here in Los Angeles where a shooting occurred just two days ago leaving a young, African American woman in critical condition. No suspects have been named in this case but police have released the name and a photo of the victim in this senseless shooting. Police say the victim is twenty-five year old Keshawn Flower of South Los Angeles, California."

A picture of KeKe covered the TV screen with the number to call if you had any information regarding the case. The news reporter continued on saying, "If anybody knows anything about this horrible incident we urge you to contact the Los Angeles Police Department. Here in Los Angeles this is…"

"Aye, ain't that that bitch from that shit with Keyontay?" one of the inmates asked his patna.

"Yup, that's her. And she the same bitch Keyontay said killed that little girl."

"Real wrap? He told them boys that shit?"

"That's what people are sayin'. He did it just last week," he said as-a-matter-of-factly.

TG couldn't believe his ears. His ears had to be playin' games on him, especially with all of this tragic information hitting him all at once. He was on an emotional rollercoaster and couldn't believe what he'd just heard. His heart was crushed, his mind wandered back and forth between thoughts of KeKe, his daughter, and these two assholes that sat just across the way from him. On any other occasion he would have stomped a mud hole in their asses but today was unbelievably different. Because of his worries about his family he couldn't even find the energy to throw them thangs. But, make no mistake, he wanted to with everything in him and would do just that when the time was right. For the moment they were the least of his concern. The life of the one woman he'd ever loved was now in jeopardy and he had to figure some things out. The two inmates had no idea what they had just done. Completely unaware of their surroundings they had fucked up and gotten their friend a death sentence.

ðð̃ð̃

"Aye homie, pass me that towel off my bunk real fast," Keyontay said holding his hand out waiting to receive the towel from his cellie. After grabbing the towel firmly in his hand, he turned around headed out the cell and to the showers. Only three feet from the cells entrance, an inmate roughly bumped into him causing him to stumble.

"What the...," before he could finish his sentence he found himself moaning and groaning in agony while staring into the eyes of his assailant through bulging eyes.

A shooting pain struck through his abdomen from the repeated stab wounds and all he could do was take it. His hands gripped his stomach as blood gushed through his fingertips dripping down onto the tiers floor and staining the shoes he bore on his feet. His body became limp and fell to the floor and just as it did that same shooting pain was released into his shoulder. The shank had ripped through his neck at least two times causing serious damage to his larynx. His attacker moved swiftly down the tier and his cellie followed suit, neither of them wanting to be anywhere near the scene when the deputies arrived. When they did, it marked the beginning of a whole lot of problems and one of the longest lockdowns this jail had ever experienced.

Chapter Six

At home, Mai was beginning to wonder why her Mommie wasn't picking her up or calling the way she usually did. For the first time since she could remember, this was the first time her mom had ever missed a night at home. And for Mai that was a problem. Her stomach told her that something was terribly wrong and her mother taught her that her stomach will never lie to you. From what she was told, her mom was in the hospital sick and Mai knew in her heart that that wasn't enough to stop her mother from calling. Their relationship was closer than close and KeKe always let her daughter know that nothing but death could ever change that. So why wasn't she calling? What could be going on? Mai laid in her bed, curled up with her hands gently laying under her face, wondering if anybody was ever gonna tell her the truth.

"Mai! Time to eat mama," Niece yelled from the kitchen.

Mai wasn't sure if she even wanted to eat at this point. Besides, the way her stomach was twisted right now, she was liable to throw up all of her insides if she ate. When she failed to come into the kitchen to eat, Niece entered her room ready to demand she do so. The sight of her niece lying there looking sad immediately changed her approach.

Her voice softened and she sat beside her on the edge of the bed, "Mai, what's wrong baby," she asked while stroking her hair back.

Tears began to trickle down her face from one side to the other. She never said a word, just laid there silently, thinking of the possibilities of what was going on.

"Mai, talk to me. Why the sad face and the tears?"

Still not getting any response, Niece decided to ask what she had assumed all along. "Is this about your Mom?"

Mai shifted her eyes in her direction and stared at her as if to say, what the fuck you think.

"I'm sure she'll be home soon, okay? Come on and wash your face so that you can eat," she said patting Mai on her hip, preparing to make way for the kitchen. Mai was furious. Nobody understood just how smart and grown up Mai really was. What happened next would come as a total shock to Niece and leave her in a difficult position.

"Then why hasn't she called? Why haven't y'all called her for me? If all she is, is sick then what is the problem?"

Mai was now sitting in an upward position looking into her aunt's eyes waiting to hear the response she would give. Just as she expected, her aunt sat in silence looking at Mai in a state of shock. This only made things worse because now Mai was forced to take it a step further.

"Well take me to go see her and I can see for myself! She tells me everything so I know for a fact she'll tell me herself what is going on." Mai was serious as a heart attack and began putting her shoes on. When she reached for her coat that hung a few feet away from her on the pink and white coat hanger, Niece grabbed her by the arm and asked her to sit down. This was about to be the hardest thing she'd ever done but knew she had no other choice.

"Mai," she paused for a long time trying to gather the right words to say, "Your Mom was shot and she was hurt pretty bad."

Tears began flowing freely from Mai's eyes as she shook her head in disbelief but Niece continued on.

"The only reason we haven't taken you to see her is because she didn't want you to see her like that."

Mai knew her last statement was untrue because her Mom would never deny her daughter the chance to see her and hear firsthand what happened, why, and how she plans to fix it. Her Mom was always like that. Sure her Mom was out in the streets a lot but she made sure Mai understood that Mommie had to pay bills. She understood that Mommie wasn't gonna rest until Mai, home, and her family was taken care of. KeKe's parenting skills had paid off tremendously because Mai was sharper than a tack. She was always honest with her daughter when things were good and bad, she explained things to her in as much detail that was needed to help her understand her

41

reasoning, and each and every time she came home Mai got her undivided attention; real quality time with her Mother. This was KeKe's way of teaching Mai what real life consisted of. Although there were things that KeKe would never expose her to directly, she insisted on exposing her to it indirectly; be it verbally or through her life's experiences.

"You're lying! Take me to see my Mom right now." Mai demanded just as upset as she was a few moments ago.

"Mai, baby," Niece spoke in a soft tone placing her hand on Mai's shoulder, bending down to look into her hurt-filled eyes. Mai snatched away, pushing past her headed out the door.

"I'll be waiting in the car."

Niece couldn't believe this was happening right now. This little girl act just like her damn Mama. And if she was right, this trip to the hospital was far from debatable. Mai's mind was made up and the only way to prevent an even bigger argument, someone better get to movin' now. Before she did, she made a call to the hospital to confirm whether or not it would be okay for Mai to see her. When the nurses gave her the okay she hung up the phone, grabbed her jacket and headed out the door only to find Mai sitting in the front seat of her Mom's car with her arms crossed, seat belt on, and tears rolling down her face. Niece decided to just get in the car and drive. The whole trip was taken in complete silence. The closer they got to the hospital the heavier Niece's heart became. This was something that would change Mai's life forever. She couldn't imagine going through what this little girl was about to experience. Thoughts of her brother's death crossed her mind and she remembered the hurt, the pain, the rage, and the emptiness she felt. She didn't want this for her niece. No kid should ever have to experience this. It was bad enough her father was in jail. Now KeKe's ass is on the verge of being gone too. This was extremely too much.

Niece began to wonder if Mai was experiencing the same heaviness and nervousness she was. When they pulled up in the parking lot and parked, her answer to that question came quick. Mai unbuckled her seat belt and charged towards the sliding doors marked EMERGENCY. Niece hadn't even turned off the ignition yet and Mai was outta there. She turned the car off and jumped out the car.

"Mai!"

She raced towards her in an attempt to stop her. When she caught up to her she was already at the desk asking to see her Mom. To make matters worse, Lea, her little sister, was there too. Confused, Niece asked, "What the…. How did you get here?"

"I caught the bus."

"The bus, why the hell would you do that? Does Mama know where you are?"

"No."

"Oh my god, she is gonna beat yo' ass. What were you thinking?"

"I needed to see KeKe. Everybody actin' like I'm a little baby and don't want to tell me what's goin' on so I came to see for myself."

Mai looked at her then back at Niece like, *yeah, what she said.* The nurse had already given Lea her visitors pass and was now looking on the list to find Mai's name.

"I'm sorry but there's no Maiesha on the list," the nurse said sympathetically.

"There has to be a mistake, Niece said to the lady while at the same time watching Mai's reaction to what she'd just said.

"It's not here. You can try to contact the family to get it resolved but at this moment I can't allow her to go in."

Mai was furious and began losing control. Her loud shouts of anger could be heard throughout various parts of the hospital. Papers and other things that occupied the countertop was knocked to the floor, and the only thing that could calm her down was seeing her mother.

"You know what, forget this!" Mai snatched the visitors tag off of Niece's shirt and ran down the hall counting down the numbers along the wall as she passed them until finally reaching her mother's room. The door was open so she walked right in and came face-to-face with her worst nightmare. She suddenly moved in slow motion, looking confused and heartbroken all at the same time. Tubes were coming out and going through every hole imaginable, machines were beeping, and KeKe lay motionless. Niece, Lea, and the nurse from the front desk came barging into the room yelling her name, but was already too late. By the time they made their entrance in an attempt to stop her, she was slumped over the bed with her head lying on her mother's chest.

"Mommie, what happened? Get up please." Her head never lifted from her chest as she spoke softly to her mother, caressing her as she pleaded. "You are all I have. Please! Just get up. Nobody is telling me anything and you promised we will never have any secrets. I'm a big girl like I said I would be. I'm ready to hear whatever you have to tell me. I just want you to wake up, Mom." No one in the room could believe how maturely she was handling things. The words coming out of her mouth was nothing like those of a ten year old kid. She sounded more like she was trying to console her mother herself. The nurse decided to let them be and exited the room to occupy her post. As she walked out, Loc walked in and almost passed out when he seen Mai lying on her mom.

"Who brought her up here?" he asked upset, but calmly speaking. Niece tried to take him outside to talk to him, but Mai beat her to the punch.

"Uncle Loc, can you tell me what happened to my mom?" Her eyes were filled with hurt and overflowing with tears. Loc asked Niece and Lea to leave the room so they could talk and they did.

"Come here," Loc said sitting down on the auburn colored chair with his arms spread open for her to come here. She jumped down off of the bed and ran to him hugging him tighter than she ever had. "Look Mai," he said wiping the tears from her eyes, "I'm not gone lie to you, your Mom was shot and they hurt her pretty badly. Things might look real bad right now but she gone be okay. She's the strongest person we know. There's no way she's goin out like this," he assured her.

Queen B. G.

Mai raised her head from off of his chest and looked him in his eyes, "Thanks," she said softly. She felt a sense of relief because at least now she knew what was wrong. And unlike everyone else, she believed her mom was gonna be just fine. Nothing and no one could change her mind. "Uncle Loc," she began speaking. Loc lifted his head as to say what's up. "Do you know who did it?" Loc shook his head hurt by the fact that the person who did this was still unknown. "Well when you find 'em, are you gone kill 'em?" she asked just as serious as a heart attack. Loc couldn't believe his ears, but smiled inside because this was definitely KeKe all over again. Before he could answer Mai made another statement. "I think you should kill 'em cause it will make me and my Mommie feel a lot better."

"Don't talk like that. You let us grownups worry about all of that and you just worry about being the best daughter you can be. Okay?"

Mai shook her head and asked a question that no one seemed to think about the entire time this has been going on.

"Well where is D? Does he know who did it?" And just like that a light bulb came on in Loc's head and he kissed Mai on the forehead saying, "As a matter of fact I'm about to handle him right now," and out the door he went to do some damage control.

Chapter Seven

5:30a.m. and Kai was sitting her ass in the holding tank nervous, frustrated, and cold as a muthafucka. Court doesn't start until about nine o'clock, so why they wake them up so early is still a mystery to everyone in attendance. There are about twenty-five inmates occupying the small, stuffy room. Some sat in chill mode while others were excited to be accompanied by some of their loved ones who had also found themselves caught up in this cruel, fucked up system. Kai didn't know what to expect and due to her sister's unfortunate circumstance. She feared the worst and prayed for the best. Worst case scenario was she would be spending a lot more time fighting her case from the jail facility she now called home. Best case, the police would hold up to their end of the bargain and send her home real soon.

After an hour of listening to people rant and rave about their cases and their enemies, a deputy walked in with a couple of papers in his hands. Everyone turned to face the large framed, chocolate toned brotha as he began to saturate the room with his deep, sexy tone of voice calling out the last names of the inmates that were highlighted on the first page of the papers he held along with the last two numbers of their booking number. Amongst those called was Kai and she was anxious to get this show on the road. She didn't know why they were calling names so early but she was appreciative of it, none the less.

"If your name was called, today is your lucky day. Roll your property up. You're going home." Kai couldn't believe that this was really happening. She had her shit together and ready to go in a matter of minutes.

"Is he serious?" she asked one of the women whose name was also called. "Can he really do this?"

The woman looked at her just as confused as she was, "Shit I don't know but he said we goin' so I'm gone."

Kai thought about using the phone to call someone to pick her up but decided against it. Not only did she want her release to be a surprise but she also needed time to elaborate on the story she would tell everyone who asked about her release. She knew they would ask and didn't know how she would answer the question considering she didn't fully understand how it happened her damn self. The releasing process took a lot longer than she anticipated, but when she walked out and got a breath of fresh air she was ecstatic. Her eyes were very sensitive to the sun causing her to squint a little and cup her hand over her eyes as if it were a sun visor. Though her eyes may have been sensitive, her skin could really use some help from the sunlight. She had gotten at least two shades lighter since being locked up and her glow was completely gone. She was now just as pale as Casper the Friendly Ghost and refused to remain that way. With taxi cabs lined along the curbside and a few dollars in her pocket she decided to just catch a cab home. A smile spread across her face as she imagined her daughter being in her arms once again. She thought of all the things they would do together to make up for the time she was away. Also on her mind was her husband and how tremendously helpful and supportive he had been during her incarceration. She planned to wait on him hand and foot and sex him like he'd never been sexed before. Spending time in a facility full of women had taught her some things. Her inner freak was waiting to break loose and was sure to have Bo sprung. Just thinking about it had her pussy tingling, becoming moist, and saturating her panties. Had it not been for the taxi driver in the car with her she would have masturbated the whole way home.

"We've reached your destination ma'am," the cab driver said looking at Kai through his rearview mirror, smiling as he realized he had just interrupted what could have been an orgasm in the back seat of his car.

Kai was startled and replied with a bit of nervousness, "Oh. Thanks. How much do I owe you?"

"That'll be $39.50." the cab driver said.

Kai looked at him like he was crazy, "Fort…. Did you just say almost forty dollars?" she asked him.

The cab driver shook his head yes.

"Let me go get some more money for you real quick. This shit don't make no damn sense." Kai exited the car after passing him the twenty-eight dollars she did have in her possession and slammed the door, mumbling as she walked down the walkway leading to her house. The lawn was trimmed to perfection just as the trees and bushes were that occupied the yard. New patio furniture occupied the porch leaving an attractive but comfortable feel to the home. There was a Dodge Charger SRT8 in the driveway that she assumed was Bo's or maybe even a rental. Just as she started to knock on the door she remembered she had her keys. Once she entered the house she saw that new furniture had been added to the living room and the sweet smell of pomegranate and berries filled the air.

Harmony's voice was coming from the kitchen, laughing and giggling like she was having fun. Kai tip toed around the corner to join in on the fun and found her daughter at the breakfast table with an unknown woman, both in their pajamas.

"What the... Who the hell are you and why are you in my house?" Kai asked with her hands on her hips.

"Mommie!" Harmony jumped down out of her chair and ran over to her mother with her arms stretched out to hug her.

Instead of hugging her Kai grabbed her by the arm, "Wait a minute baby," pushing Harmony over to the side.

"Who the fuck are you?" she asked again, this time making her way towards the woman. Just as the woman was about to answer the question, Kai was close enough to go for the kill, and raised her hand to smack the woman. But, it never happened. Bo stood right behind her, catching her arm in mid stride. This made her furious.

"Boy! You better get yo hands off of me. You protectin' this bitch?"

"Baby, calm down, it's not what you think."

Still struggling to break away from his hold Kai said, "It ain't what I think? This bitch in MY house wit' some muthafuckin' pajamas on at seven o' clock in the mornin', laughin' and gigglin' wit' my muthafuckin' daughter and it's not what I think? I ought to beat both of y'all ass."

"If you calm down I can explain," Bo assured her but she wasn't trying to hear it. All she wanted was an opportunity to get ahold of the woman she assumed was trying to take her place.

"Harmony, go to your room," she yelled. As Harmony ran off, she cried heavily wondering why this was happening. "Now let me go. I swear to god you got me fucked up. I'ma stomp a mud hole in her ass, you watch, and you better be gone before I finish because yo ass is next."

She fought long and hard to break free and still it wasn't working. Bo grew tired of her tantrum and for the first time in his life he slapped the shit out of her.

"Now calm the fuck down so I can talk, shit. This is the muthafuckin' babysitter stupid. If you listen sometimes instead of bein' all ignorant and ghetto like that you wouldn't have this problem."

The babysitter stood just a few feet away shocked at what just happened. She had been watching Harmony for a little over two months now and has never seen Bo so much as raise his voice. He was so calm and cheerful that she sometimes found herself wishing her father was that way. The person he had turned into now was a bit much for her to handle. She was afraid of him and made a mental note to never get on his bad side.

Kai stood in an awkward position, still held captive by Bo's strong hold, and took in what he'd just said. "The babysitter?"

"Yeah, the babysitter. I was on my way out to work."

"So what the babysitter spends the night and shit too," Kai asked a little more calm than before. "She got pajamas on and shit."

"No ma'am. Since I have to be here so early in the morning I just get dressed over here. I'm sorry if that's a problem."

"Don't be silly Tamika. It's no problem at all," Bo said assuring her that nothing has changed. "Can you go in the room and check in on Harmony? My wife and I have some talking to do."

Without any words in exchange, Tamika moved slowly from the corner she occupied in the far corner of the kitchen and cautiously slid past Kai to do as she was told. Immediately after she was out of arms reach Bo released his hold on Kai and demanded that she sat down. Realizing that she had already fucked up once, she sat down at the kitchen table and listened to what her husband had to say.

"You need to check yourself. I work two jobs to hold this shit down and Harmony is well taken care of in the process. That little girl is only eighteen years old and you think that I would fuck with her? What I look like bringing a bitch up in here and having her all in my daughter's life like we one big happy family? Harmony knows who her mama is. And then you push her away to get to another bitch like she's nothing. I should slap yo ass again," he said mad as hell at Kai's actions.

"Now hold on, you ain't gone do no more slapping up in here. You got away wit' the first one. The next one gone write you a check yo ass can't cash."

"I will…. You know what, never mind. Go in there and holla at my daughter like a momma is supposed to. I'm not about to go through this macho shit wit' you. And apologize to Tamika too," he said while grabbing his things to go to work. Kai had him so furious that he mumbled all the way out the front door. "Bitch done did a couple of months in the county and think she harder than paint. Done lost her muthafuckin' mind." Then the door slammed.

Kai stood in the center of the living room feeling real bad about the drama she had caused. What was supposed to be a reunion filled with happiness and love was destroyed. Instead it was an addition to the pain and disappointment that she had already bestowed on her family. Her presence had caused her husband to leave the house completely unprepared for a full day of courtesy and respect for others. With the attitude he had, they were up Shit's creek when it comes to good customer service skills. Even Harmony was a bit aggravated by her presence. She missed her mother deeply but never had a day that caused her any pain or sadness. Her father made sure that all of her days were bright days that would one day be even brighter by her mom coming home. Now that she had, Harmony erased all of the possibilities of a bright day and vowed to treat her mother just as ugly as she had treated Tamika.

Kai knew of her daughter's sadness but decided to give her some space. Instead of consoling her, she headed to the bathroom to draw some water for a long awaited bath. Once the water was running and the temperature was warm to touch, she went to her room for some underwear and a nice, but comfortable outfit. Within minutes she decided on a red and white velour outfit and placed it at the foot of the bed. The sun gave off a beautiful glow; shining at just the right angle to send off a slight flicker from the rhinestones displayed across the front of the jacket. Her Victoria's Secret underwear was tossed on top of it complimenting the outfit. Trimmed with red stitching and a few hearts made of rhinestones, it was a perfect match.

The bath water was finally ready and Kai stood beside the tub slowly undressing. Her movement alone suggested she had a lot on her mind. She extended her right leg over the tub using her big toe to test the water. It wasn't as warm as she would have liked, but she decided to get in anyway. One leg after the other was placed into the cool water and then her waist until finally she was covered to her neck with water. Her head tilted back resting along the lining of the tub. Her eyes closed. Then like a movie all of her thoughts played continuously in her mind causing a tear to slowly roll down her face.

This was the moment of truth. With no one around to distract her or try and better her situation she was forced to deal with the thoughts of what today would bring. She had already upset her husband, scared the shit out of the babysitter, and hurt her daughter's feelings. Now it was time to face her family and friends, explain what happened with her case, and go see her sister in the hospital. All of this was too much. Instead of a relaxing bath she found herself feeling like she was having an anxiety attack. Desperately wanting to get her mind off of this and on to something else she quickly bathed and got dressed hoping the sound of music and some breakfast would change the mood.

Unfortunately for her that didn't work. Harmony was locked up in her room refusing to come out and just as she sat at the table to eat her oatmeal and toast there was a knock at the front door.

"Who is it?" Kai yelled mad that her breakfast was interrupted.

"It's me, Niece. Open the door Tamika I have to use the bathroom."

Hearing those words only made Kai more frustrated. It reminded her of the ass she had made of herself moments ago. The door opened and Niece went crazy.

"Ahhhh! Sis, you're home," she said jumping up and down hugging Kai like she had been gone forever.

Kai felt good now that she knew she was truly missed, but couldn't seem to shake the disappointment she felt from the previous mishaps.

"Hey sis!"

"Girl I can't believe that you're home. Are you okay? When did you get here? Why didn't you tell anybody?" The questions just kept on coming and Kai just smiled.

"Calm down Niece, dang," she laughed while leading her sister to the kitchen sitting down next to her at the table. "I'm fine. I got out this morning and decided to surprise everybody so…Surprise!"

"So what's up now? I mean, is this shit over and done with or what?"

Kai knew this question would come sooner or later. She just kinda hoped it would be later. "Yup, it's over," Kai said full of relief.

"So what did they say?"

"They gave me a DA reject." Niece looked at her confused so Kai continued on to explain. "They basically saying they don't have enough evidence to charge me so they're letting me go."

"But wait. I thought they said they had a lot of evidence against you."

"Girl, you know the police lie."

"Well, I'm just happy that it's all over and that you are back home. I know Harmony was ecstatic huh? She missed you so much."

"Yeah well, she's not really talking to me right now."

"What you mean not talkin' to you? What happened?" Kai went on to explain to Niece what happened when she came home and Niece just shook her head. "Kai, what were you thinking? Tamika is like a big sister to Harmony. They do everything together and you done did some dumb shit like that?"

"You're right but I didn't know," Kai said sadly. "I just, I don't know man, fuck."

"Let me go check on my niece."

Seeing that the door was locked Niece knew for a fact that Harmony was angry. She knocked on the door several times and Harmony never said a word. Nor did she attempt to open the door. Kai shrugged her shoulders and sat back at the table to continue her food which was now cold.

"Harmony, it's Auntie baby, open the door."

Harmony leaped off the bed, opened the door, and jumped into her aunt's arms.

"Hey pretty girl. Whatcha doin' in here?"

"Nothing."

"Why weren't you answering the door then? You don't want to see your auntie?"

"Yes. But I don't want to see Mommie."

"Hey! Don't you say that. That's not nice."

"It's not nice what she did either," Harmony stated with her arms crossed.

Niece did all that she could to reason with her niece before picking out some clothes for her to get dressed in. She figured she would go ahead and take Harmony with her as planned and give her mom some time to work things out. Once

Harmony was dressed and ready to go, they left the house to have some fun. Still, Harmony never said a word to her mother.

One Year Later

Chapter Eight

Almost a year had gone by and things were as complicated as they were around the same time the previous year. Harmony was still resenting her mom, Bo is tired of her bullshit as well, KeKe is still in the hospital with no sign of improvement, TG is still in the shoe program as a result of the attack against Keyontay, and Loc, along with Mai, is still at KeKe's bedside on a regular basis; praying, talking and sharing happy memories of their past. Even Charmaine came to the hospital to visit KeKe. No one had seen or heard from her in months and when she made her first appearance at the hospital, Loc didn't even recognize who she was. She had gained at least thirty pounds, her hair was long and beautiful, her make-up was flawless and she dressed as if she worked in corporate America. Loc couldn't believe his eyes, but shook his head in approval, smiling at the progress she'd made. Just as she promised, she'd checked herself into rehab and was now eleven months clean and sober. When she found out about the terrible shooting involving KeKe, it ripped her heart to shreds. While lying in her bed on many different occasions she prayed and asked God to cover KeKe and give her another chance at life. She promised herself that as soon as they released her from the program she was going to see her and she did. A part of her believed that if KeKe could hear out of her own mouth that she was clean and sober, ready and willing to give that same love and support that was always given to her, and praying for her full but speedy recovery, that she would find the strength to wake up out of this. For hours she sat at KeKe's bedside praying, smiling, and caressing her hair.

"God, if you can bring me outta my mess then I KNOW you can bring her out of this. I trust you Lord to do your work and I claim it done right now. In Jesus name…. AMEN."

After those last words, Charmaine leaned down to kiss KeKe's forehead and headed out the door to find out what she could do to help Mai. Even if no help was needed, she was determined to establish a relationship with Mai and uphold her promise to pay KeKe back for all the love, respect, and care that she gave her and her daughter even through her addiction. KeKe was the only person in the world that still treated her like a human being and Charmaine was forever grateful for that. It was something that she took note of and would always carry deep in her heart.

Kai, on the other hand, had been to the hospital once since her release and never went again. No one understood her reasoning behind it but many believed that maybe it was just the fact that she didn't want to see her sister that way. No one knew of the secret she kept. At least that's what she thought.

While driving down Broadway with his music bumpin', windows cracked allowing the cool breeze to brush against his face, and a fly little lady in his passenger seat, Ridah caught a glimpse of his little homegirl shaking hands with a man he'd seen her with on several occasions. Only this time the man in question had mistakenly allowed his badge to remain visible at his waist line.

"This nigga is the police," he said out loud causing his lady friend to take a look herself.

Ridah had seen her going in and coming out of the police station a few times and began to wonder what she was up to. He never approached her out of respect for her family but had come to the point where something had to be said. His plan to enjoy this day while making a little money in the process had quickly changed. His focus was now on some real live hood business and everything else had to wait; including the young lady in his passenger seat that was now irritated by the realization that she was on her way back home. Ridah had already bust a U-turn and was headed back to her crib to drop her off. Had he been anyone else, she would have gotten smart, but with Ridah it was a whole 'nother ball game. A smart mouth would get her ass slapped and kicked to the curb quicker than she could blink her eyes. Yeah, he was cool, but they called him Ridah for a reason. His hood and his loved ones came before any and everything life had to offer. When the streets called, he went running and when it was time for hood politics, he was the first to stand up for what he represented.

ððð

"Aye, my nig. What's up?"

"Awe, not too much. What's goin' on wit' you?"

"Shit, in traffic. We need to holla homie on some real shit and I think you need to call the squad so we can round table 'bout some shit."

"Is that right? Well what's up? We need to bring that shit out or what?" Big Rocco asked referring to the guns he had waiting on anybody that chose to get out of line.

"Naw, this our home team we talkin' 'bout. I'll put y'all up on game about it and then you can handle it from there."

"I can handle it? Cuz, where you at?"

"On my way to you. I'll be there in less than twenty."

The call was ended and Ridah was pushing through traffic. Disappointment was written all over his face and for the first time, he questioned the integrity of one of his own. Prior to this situation, he was confident that the closest people to him were thorough breed and would remain solid till the death of them. No one in his immediate circle or his 'family' for that matter has ever flopped on anything. He wished with all of his heart that it hadn't changed now. His heart was heavy and his head began to hurt as he thought to himself, *Right is right and wrong is wrong. Please don't say she foul like this because I never wanted to have to give a green light on none of mines.* Just as he found himself thinking that, he planned on repeating those very words to the rest of the crew when they sat at the roundtable.

ððð

Knock Knock Knock.

The door was half open and gave off a sound of hollowness when being tapped on. No one in the house moved but looked to one another in hopes that someone would volunteer to get the door.

"Who is it?" Pookie yelled while walking towards the door.

"It's Ridah, Cuz. Open the door."

The door flung open to their hideaway and in walked Ridah with a look of disappointment on his face, followed by Loc and Moe. His body language spoke volumes and the crew couldn't wait to see what this was all about. With everybody present, all of the men walked simultaneously down the hallway and took their seat at the table in the black room. The black room, which was also the dining room, was decorated with all black everything; the carpet, the oversized round onyx table, plush suede chairs, and the crystal frames that held the photos that lined the walls throughout the room were all black and very expensive. The room itself had a value of at least $500,000.00 dollars.

"I can't believe I'm about to say this," Ridah said sitting in his chair rubbing his hand across his head as if he were very irritated. "Pookie, you and my nigga Rocco are like brothers to me. We been together since we were knee high to a frog. You know I'm not wit' the funnies and wouldn't be a part of nothing I wasn't sure about. I think Kai is foul Cuz."

Pookie instantly got angry and jumped up from his seat to challenge Ridah for the bullshit he had just said. Rocco jumped up also, only he did so to intervene.

"Hold up, hold up, hold up," he yelled pushing Pookie back to his seat. "Hear Cuz out. If he thinks this then we definitely need to know what's up."

Pookie was pissed and had no intentions on entertaining this bullshit. However, since Rocco was so adamant about them listening and he couldn't beat him anyway, he decided to chill out. When he calmed down Rocco gave Ridah the signal to continue.

"Pookie, my nigga, we on the same team. The only reason I'm bringing it to the table is because y'all are my folks and I would rather give y'all a chance to handle it before the hood gets wind and address the situation. I done seen Kai with this dude on several occasions, seen her coming and going at the police station, and today when I saw them, Cuz still had his badge on. I don't know what you get out of that but to me that spells trouble."

"You right but I think she probably up there about KeKe. You know how close they are and we still don't know who did the shit. Give us that much. Ain't none of my folks no snitches and ain't gone be," Rocco said matter-of-factly.

"I'm wit' Rocco on this one, Cuz," Loc said shaking his head while Moe just sat in silence.

"Aye Moe Cuz, how you feel about this shit?" Ridah asked.

Still Moe said nothing and just shook his head.

"Don't shake your head. Tell us what's on your mind."

"Man, I seen that shit too homie but I thought I was trippin'. I was wit' baby 'bout to get on the freeway and seen her get an envelope from the dude and get in her car. I feel like Rocco though, that shit has to be because of KeKe."

"Alright then it's over. Do what you gotta do to find out what's up and make sure you do it before anybody else get wind of this shit and it get out of control," Ridah said to Rocco with a pound and a warm embrace.

When Rocco walked out so did Pookie and Loc, leaving Moe to accompany Ridah. Still a little uneasy about the situation, Ridah looked at Moe and said, "Watch her ass homie. That's family but, if that bitch makes any wrong moves you better down that bitch. If she's workin' wit' the team then she gotta go."

Chapter Nine

Knock, Knock, Knock.

`Charmaine stood on the porch awaiting an answer from one of the sisters. From what she was told, Niece had been at the house holding it down since KeKe's been gone. No one answered the door so she knocked again. This time a little bit harder than the last. Unfortunately, there was still no answer and she felt disappointed. Just as she walked down the steps and headed down the walkway, a car pulled up into the driveway. Because of the angle of the sun, she was unable to get a clear view of the person occupying the car. Once the ignition was turned off and the driver emerged from the car, Charmaine noticed it was Niece. She had grown to be a beautiful young lady. Niece approached the porch with bags of groceries dangling from each of her hands and the keys hanging from her lips.

Charmaine walked towards her to offer her assistance and Niece accepted but looked at her puzzled. With one of her hands free from baggage she took the keys from her mouth, "Umm... Thank you but do I know you?"

Charmaine laughed and replied, "You really don't remember me? It's Charmaine. Bianca's mom," she said while making hand gestures.

"Charmaine? Is that really you?"

"Yup. In the flesh and at my best." Charmaine twirled around in a circle with her arms held out and ended with her hands on her hips.

"OMG, you look so beautiful. I didn't even recognize you with all them hips and stuff. KeKe would be so proud of you."

"Thank you. I've been by the hospital to see her a couple of times. If there is anything I can do to help you guys through this just let me know."

"Aww thanks girl. I appreciate it. Well come on in and sit down," she said opening the door and heading towards the kitchen.

"I see you're doing a damn good job keeping the house together."

"I try. After all that KeKe has done for me, it's the least I could do."

"For you? You mean for all of us. That girl is nothing but a blessing in disguise."

"I know right. I wish more people looked at it that way."

"What you mean?"

"Girl, you know how it is. Out of sight out of mind. I know it's been over a year since the shooting happened, but no one comes by here to say how you doing, do you need anything, or nothing. The only person still going to the hospital is Loc. I mean, don't get me wrong, I don't need nobody, but Mai is wondering why everybody disappeared the way they did. All of these people KeKe looked out for while she was here and not one of them people are looking out for us now that she's gone." Niece began shaking her head and the anger that was building up inside was written all over her face. Even her body language had changed.

"I understand how you feel but that's exactly why I came over here. I want to help you with Mai in any way that I can. I know how hard it is to be a teenage mother and if you don't mind, I want to lift that burden off of you."

"Thanks Charmaine, but I don't know," she said with her face slightly twisted. "I appreciate it, but you have your own issues to deal with. No disrespect."

"None taken. I understand, but I promise you that I'm better now. I'm not the person I use to be and I can assure you that I'm fully capable of fulfilling this task. Not only am I clean, but I'm spiritually and mentally rehabilitated. You can trust me," she said in an attempt to reassure Niece that she could be trusted.

Niece believed her and could look into her eyes and see down in her soul. She was really a brand new person. For hours they sat conversing about nothing in particular and had a ball doing so. The more Niece talked to her, the closer they became and it went on and on for days. She would come by on a regular basis just to see how things were going and to take Mai on play dates at the park and things of that nature. Mai enjoyed it too. It was something she had begun looking forward to every day. Niece found herself loving the freedom that came from the help Charmaine provided and began wondering to herself just how good it would be for her to take over and allow her to have her childhood back.

ðð̃ð

Something about being at the hospital today felt different. Loc couldn't quite put his finger on what it was, but hoped it meant something good. After pulling the curtains open to let the sunshine penetrate the room, he stood over KeKe and said, "Aye baby, it's a beautiful day outside. It sho would be nice to have my home-girl enjoying it with me today."

Loc knew he wouldn't get any type of response, but enjoyed talking to her as if nothing was wrong. It was his way of keeping hope alive and motivating her to get up. That is, if she could hear him, of course. Just as he began to embrace this unusually good feeling, a nurse walked in and shattered his feelings and his heart. "Sir, we're gonna have to ask you to leave now."

Loc was confused. They never had a problem with him being there before. What made today so different he wondered. "Why? Is something wrong?"

"The family has decided to take her off of life support."

"Hold on...... what? Hell naw! I will pay for this shit for as long as I have to but y'all are not about to take her off of shit." Loc was angry as hell and losing his self-control. This was his first time hearing of this and he wasn't ready to face the fact that his loc was about to be gone forever. He began pacing back and forth with tears streaming freely down his face. His anger frightened the young nurse.

"I'm sorry about this, but I'm only doing my job. The family made the decision early this morning." She began moving things out of her way to begin doing as she was told to.

"Wait! Damn it, now wait!" he yelled while pounding his fist down on the table. "The family can't make no decision like that without the whole family. This is my sister. Let me talk to them before you do anything. Please lady. Just give me twenty-four hours to change their minds. Please?" he said looking at the nurse through evil, but hurting eyes. If she did this, it would not only kill KeKe, but kill him also. He would literally have a nervous breakdown if she carried this out.

The nurse saw the pain in his eyes and decided to go take it up with her superior. "I can't make that type of decision, but I'll go talk to my supervisor to see what I can do. I'm not making any promises though."

"Thank you! Thank you!" Loc said with a sigh of relief.

When the nurse left the room Loc stood at KeKe's bedside and grabbed her hand. His heart hurt so bad that he began feeling weak. He kneeled down on one knee to avoid falling out on the floor and began talking to KeKe.

"Baby look, you gone have to get yo ass up. You hear me Cuz? Get up! Get up my nigga!" He began sobbing harder than he'd ever had. "Baby please, they are tryin' to take you from me my nigga. Did you just hear that? Don't let this happen, man. Get up!" He pulled on KeKe's arm but still she didn't budge. For the first time in his life Loc felt defeated and helpless. All he could do was hope that the doctors took what he said into consideration.

About twenty minutes later the nurse reappeared, accompanied by Dr. Tsani. He and Loc knew each other very well due to Loc's continuous visits to the hospital. They had gotten close and established a nice rapport with one another.

"This is my supervisor," the young lady stated.

"Dr. Tsani, what's up man?" Loc asked standing to his feet to embrace him. "Don't do this to me man."

"Ahhhh Mr. Jones, how's it going man? My nurse tells me that you were not aware of the actions about to take place. I'm sorry to hear that. Unfortunately, I can't just go against the family's wishes. That would jeopardize my job."

"I hear you, but you can't just give me twenty-four hours though? That's all I'm askin' man."

Dr. Tsani felt bad and sympathized with Loc. He looked as if he were gonna stick to his guns but surprised everyone when he said, "Sure. I'll give you twenty-four hours but that's it. Make sure someone contacts me regarding you guys' final decision."

With that said Loc hugged the doctor like he never had before then kissed KeKe on the forehead and headed to Shell's house.

ð ð ð

Skirrrrrrrrt!

The car came to a screeching halt and was thrown in park with so much force that the gear handle made a popping noise. The driver door flew open and was slammed closed.

BOOM!

Everyone in his immediate presence could see that something was terribly wrong and waited eagerly to find out what it was. While some feared his next move, the others was anxious to witness the latest occurrence of drama so they could run and gossip to their friends. As usual the door was unlocked so he let himself waltz right on in.

"Shell!" His voice was loud, deep, and held about as much authority as expected from a male dominant.

"What?" Shell yelled back with just as much hostility as he had.

"You takin' KeKe off life support homie? Why would you do that?"

"First of all, slow yo' roll. I ain't yo homie. Now if you wanna sit down and talk about this we can, but you gone talk to me like you got some sense."

"My bad Moms. But what's up? If it's the money, all you gotta do is tell me and I got it."

Shell took a seat next to him on the sofa and looked him in his eyes, "Son, my baby is tired. I know you don't wanna see her go, shit I don't either, but we have to. She's been through enough. It's our own selfishness that has kept her here this long and that's not cool. It's time we let her rest in peace. God is calling her home for a reason and we need to stop trying to reverse His work."

Loc looked at her like, *Who the hell are you and what did you do with Shell?* She was unusually calm and oh so spiritual all of a sudden. Any other time, you wouldn't catch her speaking about anything pertaining to God. Or to letting KeKe just die, for that matter.

"I hear you Moms, but fuck all that. I can't let you do this. Period."

"Well what do you expect me to do Loc? I mean, for real. Have you ever stopped to think about how hurtful it is for Mai to have to look at her mom in that condition on an almost daily basis?"

Those words slapped Loc straight across the face. As much as he hated to admit it, she was right. But still, he needed some time to prepare himself for this departure. "Okay! You're right. Can you at least just give me one more week? I just need time to say my good-bye's. I'll pay for the week of treatment and whatever else you need me to do."

Shell shook her head and decided to go ahead and allow it. She knew how important KeKe was to Loc and felt obligated to respect his wishes. "ONE WEEK!" she said holding one finger up in his face indicating that she was serious as a heart attack.

Loc's heart almost burst through his chest. He leaped into Shell's arms and hugged her like his life depended on it. "Thanks Mom's! I love you Cuz."

Shell smiled inside and out about the love Loc displayed for her daughter. She only hoped that this would help bring closure to his undying love for her.

Chapter Ten

"Aye Loc, where you at?"

"I'm at the house about to hit the streets, why what's up?"

"I found out where ole boy been hiding out at. And you won't believe who his patna is."

Usually Loc would be overly excited about something like this but today he just wasn't feeling it. His mind and his focus was somewhere else. "Is that right? Who is it?" Loc asked dryly.

"It was that nigga D. Can you believe that shit? After all she had done with him, this fool is the one that did it."

"Yup, I believe it. I been thinkin' that for a while now, but I ain't neva been able to catch his ass. Mai is the one that brought it to my attention."

"Well why you neva said nothing then?"

"Cause I was gone handle it myself. But enough of that, I'ma get at you a little later."

"Hold up! What up wit' you my nig? You don't wanna go serve these fools?"

"Naw man, I'm good. You can go handle that shit if you want to. I'll holla at you later though."

"Lo…" Before he could say another word the phone was hung up in his face.

Sniper sat looking at the phone receiver wondering what the hell was wrong with his homeboy. Whatever it was, was deep, because he would never pass up an opportunity like this. Especially not when it came to KeKe. He was baffled but decided he was going to do this shit whether he had to do it himself or not.

ððð

"Okay. So this where y'all at," Sniper mumbled to himself while driving past the house looking at these lame ass dudes through the limo tented windows he had put on the rental he was in. All together he counted a total of six people outside. Three were getting in their cars preparing to leave while two stood in the yard talking to the dude on the porch. Loc parked his car just a few houses down, on the corner, where he could still get a clear view of the guys getting in the car. Once the car had pulled off and out of sight, he got out of the car and began walking down the street. With a baseball cap and a hood over his head, it was hard to get a good look at his face. Since it was a bit chilly out, no one thought twice about the dude they saw walking with his hands in his pockets and shoulders slightly lifted. To them, it indicated he was cold and so were they.

While he walked past the house directly next door to his destination, the guys talked playfully amongst each other and he heard the one thing he'd been dying to know. "D, you a damn fool man," one of the guys said to the guy standing on the porch.

This was getting better and better. Not only was he about to knock these fools down, but now, he knew exactly who D was and planned on giving him an overkill. As he approached the house, the two men on the grass looked at him like he was crazy.

"Aye, y'all know where the weed at over here?"

The two dudes made an attempt to approach him, both wearing a mean mug on their faces, and found themselves regretting it.

BOOM! BOOM! BOOM! BOOM!

The two of them dropped like flies and Sniper turned towards D and released another round of shots. D moved swiftly towards the door and fell to the floor as soon as he closed it behind himself. He was shot in his ass and in his right leg. With the door closed and locked he assumed he was safe. You know what they say, when you assume you make an ass out of yourself. And that's exactly what he did.

Sniper stood on the porch and fired about twelve shots into the door and window of the house. D crawled quickly into the next room while glass went flying everywhere. Seeing as though he'd made his presence felt, Sniper tucked away his guns and ran back down the street to the car. People had already begun to surface from inside their homes to see what was going on and surprisingly, there were no sirens heard and not a cop in sight. There was one little problem though. One of the dudes from the neighborhood had taken notice of the car and was now trying to see inside. With the car running, Sniper expected something of the sort, but hoped like hell this dude wasn't about to give him any problems. If he did, he was prepared to blow his head off his shoulders.

"What's up homie?" the dude asked curious as to what was going on. Sniper gave no response just a blank stare before hopping in the car, putting the pedal to the metal.

ð ð ð

Loc entered the hospital carrying a dozen of white roses and a bouquet of balloons. As he approached KeKe's room he ran into Dr. Tsani who was happy to see him and greeted him as such.

"Hey Mr. Jones! I see everything worked out."

Other than the fictitious smile he displayed on his face, Loc failed to give any reaction or response to what the doctor had said. He simply walked in her room, sat the roses and balloons on the table at her bedside, and kissed her hand repeatedly. Tears immediately began to flow from his eyes and he begged her to wake up. Still through all the madness and the tears, KeKe lay unresponsive on the bed.

The longer he talked and got no response the angrier he became. He knew his approach was wrong but he was desperate and at this point all he cared about was having her here. He tried everything; lifting her up out of the bed, shaking her, yelling at her, idle threats. You name it he did it and still KeKe's small framed body did nothing but fall limp.

Tired of trying and exhausted from crying, Loc prepared to leave for the day. "KeKe man.... I know you can hear me. I'ma leave it alone for today, but you better wake the fuck up. You the one that said, always trust your gut, and that's what I'm doin'. You got six mo' days Cuz." He looked at her through piercing eyes as if she could see how serious he was and it would make a difference. "I love you sis."

ðͣðͣðͣ

Loc drove home in silence with the windows down allowing the cool breeze to blow freely throughout the car, resting against his skin and assisting him in staying cool, calm and collective. For a moment he had drifted off into space thinking back on all of the havoc he and KeKe had caused. He wished with everything in him that he could turn back the hands of time and delete KeKe from all of their wrongdoings. His thoughts were interrupted by the vibrating of his phone which was lying in between his seats. Driving with one hand and reaching with the other, he fumbled for a couple minutes until he felt the phone at his fingertips. Once he retrieved the phone, it displayed a total of fifteen missed calls; thirteen of them were from Sniper. Thirteen calls meant something was terribly wrong and even though he knew he couldn't handle any more traumatic rollercoaster rides, he dialed Sniper's number and braced himself for the ride.

"Hello?"

"What's up? Is everything cool or what? I was in the hospital visiting KeKe and when I got back to my car I seen you had been blowin' me up."

"Don't trip, it's cool. I handled that shit already so gone ahead and do yo thang."

Loc wondered if what he was hearing were ill feelings or if Sniper really meant what he was saying. Not that it made any difference though because Loc had absolutely no intentions on taking the conversation any further. Besides, Sniper was still alive and breathing so that's all that really mattered to him. If shit was serious or life threatening then there would be a problem, but since it's not, Loc hung up the phone and left it at that.

ð...ð

Just ten minutes after hanging up the phone, Loc bent a corner and saw police everywhere. Yellow tape accessorized the neighborhood street while women screamed at the top of their lungs in pure agony from the loss of their loved ones. From the angle he was at, Loc counted at least two dead bodies. One laid exposed for the world to see while the other was properly covered with a white sheet. Two white vans, both marked, Los Angeles County Coroner, were present at the scene parked just beyond the yellow tape. News reporters waited anxiously at the lining of the crime scene to get as much footage as they could in hopes of getting the information needed to be the first to air the unfortunate chain of events.

Meanwhile, Loc laid low and tried his best to maneuver through the streets without being harassed by the team. As he made his way through, he thought about the two short conversations he had with Sniper and realized that this was what he was talking about. He smiled to himself, both happy and impressed by the way his homeboy had handled his business. For a second, he felt a sense of happiness and relief. He knew that there were some fatalities and hoped that one of them was D. Sadly, that was not the case at all and Loc would soon find out.

Chapter Eleven

Every day after the agreement with Shell, Loc did the same thing. Each and every visit would consist of him crying, yelling, and getting extremely upset. It wasn't until Charmaine arrived that things took a turn. Loc yelled and cursed at KeKe begging her to get up. The more time that passed the more desperate he became.

"Loc, calm down," Charmaine said with her hand resting at the small of his back.

"Leave me alone Charmaine! Time is running out and she needs to get up."

"I know but you are going about this all wrong," she said softly while looking into his eyes. "Look, you can scream, yell, curse, fight; do whatever you want. None of that is gonna make the situation any better. The only thing that can and will change this baby is prayer, and a whole lot of it."

Loc looked at her so cold that you would have thought he was gonna take her life. In return she just smiled, and kept on talking to him about the works of God. At first, Loc wasn't in the mood for any of her shit and wanted her to just shut up and leave. But, the more she talked, the more he listened. The more he listened, the more he believed in what she was saying. Especially once she used her own life as an example of the miracles God can produce. Loc had watched Charmaine smoke dope, sniff powder cocaine, and turn tricks whenever she saw fit, for his whole life. There was never a time that he had seen her sober up until now and now, she was sober and living life to the fullest.

The two of them sat at KeKe's bedside, held hands and began to pray. Charmaine was really getting it in and Loc wasn't doing too bad himself. Outside of the couple of curse words that slipped out, Loc actually had a sincere, heartfelt conversation with God. Not just about KeKe but himself also. After saying, "AMEN," the two of them hugged, kissed KeKe on the forehead and agreed to meet the next day; same time, same place.

ðÐð

The next day during his normally scheduled visit to the hospital, Loc wondered if God had heard his plea. When walking into the room where KeKe laid motionless and propped up against a soft white pillow, Loc's initial reaction was to curse her out again and try and force her to wake up. No sooner than he had gotten started he heard Charmaine's voice replaying in his head, '*Loc this isn't the way to do this....*' and just like that, Loc began praying at KeKe's bedside on bended knees with his arms resting against her bed. Tears flowed from his eyes at an uncontrollable pace and rather than wipe them away, Loc allowed them to flow. Maybe these tears would provide healing for his soul. Maybe, just maybe, after the last one fell he could find the strength and understanding he needed to deal with this unfortunate situation. Especially since he would then be thinking with a clear mind and a heart not as heavy as before.

Charmaine walked in the room and found Loc on his knees having a personal conversation with God and was overjoyed. Even if KeKe didn't make it, she realized that she had at least introduced God to another one of His children and she was very pleased with that. And Loc, of all people. Most people on the outside looking in would think of it as impossible and wouldn't dare try instilling the works of God in him but Charmaine was a true soldier of God and would proclaim her testimony to anyone who had ears to listen.

While Loc closed his prayer, Charmaine sat silently watching, laying her sweater across the tabletop and sitting her Michael Kors purse just beside it. When Loc arose from his knees, Charmaine greeted him with a huge smile and a warm embrace.

"Hey Loc. It's good to see you. How are you doing today?"

"Aw I'm good, just doing my part in these last days of seeing my dog."

Charmaine maintained her smile and nodded her head in agreement.

"I just hope he hears me you know? A nigga done did so much wrong in these streets it wouldn't surprise me one bit if God decided not to fulfill this miracle for me."

"Loc, the good thing about God is that he's not judgmental, he's not revengeful, or unapproachable. He's a forgiving God and no matter what you did in the past, it's never too late to make it right. He hears you. Trust me. He's just not on your time, he's gonna do this his way and on His time."

Loc simply shook his head as to say, *Yeah I know*, and stood there looking at his sister. Something about her appearance was calm and peaceful. Loc had never noticed this before and instantly decided that if this is where his sister was gonna find peace, then he was more than ready to accept it. He had not only grown tired of the constant pain and disappointment the streets had to offer, but he had also grown tired of seeing KeKe struggle the way she had all of her life. He wished like hell that he could have done something about it before it had gone this far, but KeKe wasn't having it. Not for a second. Everything was about money and doing it her way, on her own. The closest thing to help she was accepting was putting her up on a lick. Other than that, she didn't wanna hear it and would go ballistic if anyone overstepped that boundary and tried.

After hours of sitting around waiting for a miracle and conversing with one another, Loc and Charmaine decided to leave for the day and resume their routine tomorrow. As Loc walked out the door he stopped in his tracks and turned to Charmaine who now stood at KeKe's bedside and said," Aye Charmaine." Charmaine looked over her shoulder at him and raised her eyebrow. "Thank you," then he tapped the wall one time and disappeared down the hallway.

Charmaine smiled to herself knowing exactly what he meant then turned back to KeKe, "KeKe, I'm about to go. I don't know where you found this boy, but girl he loves you," she said referring to Loc. "I'm glad somebody does though because you deserve all the love you can handle and then some. Anyways hun, I love you and I'll see you again tomorrow, okay? Charmaine leaned down over KeKe and kissed her forehead and left the room.

ðð̃ð̃

Everyday consisted of the same things and the same two people. But unlike the earlier part of the days at this hospital, it was getting easier to deal with for Loc as opposed to becoming more difficult. He and Charmaine had developed a closeness that Loc had never anticipated. Only God knew what lay ahead of them.

ðð̃ð̃

Now here they were, down to the last day, and KeKe had still not waken up. Charmaine remained confident in what she believed would happen but Loc was beginning to think that maybe he had done too much wrong and God wasn't listening to his pleas. He paced back and forth, rubbing his head in frustration. He felt as though he was having a panic attack.

"Loc, maybe you should just have a seat. Do you want some water?"

"Naw, Charmaine. I'm cool."

"Well I am about to go down to the cafeteria to grab a little something to snack on. While I'm gone, talk to your sister. Everything you need to say, get it out now. She's listening." She winked her eye at him and made her exit.

Hours rolled by and it was nearing the time for them to leave. There would be no tomorrow. This was it. While Loc held his sister hand, he did just as Charmaine told him. He shared his deepest thoughts and feelings with her. In the midst of their one way conversation the nurse came in to begin preparing to disconnect her from the machines. Loc failed to put up a fight. This time he was gonna sit back and allow her life to take its course. Just as he was saying his final goodbyes, it happened.

"That's all I have to say sis. I love you. And just like I'm holding your hand right now, I trust that you would hold mines even from the sky."

A single tear fell from his right eye and just as he was about to walk away KeKe squeezed his hand. He thought his mind was playing tricks on him at first but something said, talk to her. And he did. "KeKe, do that again."

The nurse looked at him as if he were crazy and thought to herself, *Here we go again. This is about to be a long night.* Little did she know, Loc wasn't tripping at all. KeKe squeezed his hand again and Loc lifted her up from the pillow giving her the biggest bear hug ever. Loc laughed and cried all at the same time, excited that his only wish in the world had come true. Charmaine walked in the room, "What is going on in here?"

"She squeezed my hand Cuz. My nigga is gone make it." Loc spoke with more excitement than he ever had.

Charmaine stood frozen at the foot of the bed and said, "To God be the glory. Look at how my God works. I told you!" she smiled.

ðдð

Later that night, while walking past KeKe's room, one of the nurses overheard some noise coming from KeKe's bedroom. When she walked in she saw that KeKe was choking and trying to pull the tubes from her mouth.

"Oh shit," the nurse whispered.

This was only her second week on the job and she wasn't quite ready to deal with anything like this. "I need help in here," she yelled to anyone within earshot and tried to restrain KeKe before she killed herself.

Once the charge nurse and one of the surgeons entered the room, they first explained to KeKe how dangerous it was for her to do that, and promised her they would remove them just as soon as they could. KeKe, being the hardheaded stubborn person she was, continued to pull at the tubes. They were uncomfortable to her and as far as she was concerned, they were also the reason she couldn't breathe. Time had seemed to stand still and no one made an effort to fulfill KeKe's desire to have the tubes removed. Tears began rolling down her face, filling her earlobes because of the angle she was lying in. She fought and fought to free herself from the restraints that were now placed on her wrists and ankles to avoid hurting herself.

Dr. Tsani witnessed her constant fight and made a deal with KeKe. "Calm down, calm down. You are going to hurt yourself if you keep it up. How about you let me check your vitals and if everything is okay, I'll remove the tubes. But, you have to relax and trust me."

KeKe nodded okay and waited patiently for the doctor to access her. Her vitals were good but he was still uncomfortable about taking her off of the breathing machine. Seeing KeKe after all that she had been through, Dr. Tsani went against his better judgment and removed the tubes as KeKe requested.

"Take a deep breath for me."

ð ð ð

Ring-Ring... Ring-Ring...

"Who in the hell could this be calling at this time of night?" Shell said out loud while turning on the lamp that occupied the nightstand to the left of her bed. When the light came on she noticed the clock read 11:29 pm. Back in the day, she would have been up partying like a rock star but since KeKe had been in the hospital, all of that had changed. "Hello!" Shell yelled in the phone like she was gonna bite their head off.

"Moms!" Loc yelled right back.

"Loc? Boy what the hell do you want and why are you so damn loud?"

"Moms, KeKe gone be alright."

Before he could utter another word Shell slapped her hand down on her leg and her voice went from angry to a slight whisper. "Boy stop smokin' that shit. I don't have time for this tonight. I have to be at that damn hospital early in the morning. Now bye"

"No, Moms wait!" But, Shell had already hung up the phone.

Ring-Ring....Ring-Ring...

"Got-dammit!" Shell yelled while picking up the phone. "What!"

"Don't hang up! I was at the hospital and KeKe squeezed my hand. She squeezed my hand!"

"Loc, I ain't got time for yo shit," Shell sat up in her bed not knowing whether she should believe him or hang up on him.

"I swear Moms. Charmaine was there too. You can call the hospital if you don't believe me."

Shell dropped the phone and began screaming. She shook her husband, waking him up from his sleep. "Get up Pookie! Get up!"

"Man, what the fuck you want?" he asked irritated as hell. When he looked up Shell was smiling and crip walking all over her side of the bedroom. "What the hell is wrong with you, waking a nigga up, doing all this dumb shit, crip walkin' and shit? Take yo ass to sleep."

"My baby woke up Cuz. Yeeeeaaaaaahhhhhh!" Shell continued to dance with one sock hanging on for dear life and the other one pulled all the way up to her calves. Her hair was in two ponytails, flopping all over the place, while her fingers displayed gang signs that changed so fast that you had to be a pro to figure them out.

Pookie couldn't believe his ears and got up and out of the bed to check on it himself. He dialed the hospital, asked to speak to KeKe's nurse, and anxiously awaited her feedback. A part of him was excited, but the other part of him expected this to be one of Shell's high moments. And if it turned out to be just that, he was gonna go upside her head for waking him up with this bullshit.

"Hello, this is Nurse Simmons, how may I help you?"

"Hi, this is Mr. Flowers, Keshawn's dad, my wife got a phone call stating that she woke up, is that true?"

"Well Mr. Flowers, as much as I would like to share that information with you, I am unable to do so over the phone. You are more than welcome to come in to the hospital and speak with me or Dr. Tsani regarding her status if you'd like."

Hearing those words irritated the shit out of Pookie. Rather than lash out at her for simply doing her job, he hung up in her face and prepared to travel to the hospital to check on his daughter. Within minutes both Pookie and Shell were dressed and ready to go. Shell jumped in the driver's seat while Pookie decided to stretch out across the back seat. As they pulled away from the curbside, the windows were cracked permitting the cool air access to circulate through the car. Pookie watched from the backseat as Shell's ponytails danced in the wind and just shook his head. Shell paid him no attention at all as she swerved through the streets bumping the Eastsida's and anticipating the moment she'd see her daughter again. Unlike Pookie, she had no doubt that her daughter did in fact wake up from the long and unfortunate coma she'd been in for such a long period of time and planned on celebrating the whole way there and every day after.

When the car came to a halt in front of the hospital, Shell hopped out with the music playing loudly and began crip walking once again. She was gettin it in until Pookie emerged from the car tired of her antics.

"Shell, I'm not playin' with you Cuz. Sit yo ignorant ass down somewhere."

Shell continued to do as she was doing and completely ignored Pookie's statement. The feeling she had at this moment was like no other and this was her way of letting it out. Pookie knew that he had married a fool and that she was always extra but right now he wasn't in the mood for her shit. Instead of yelling or repeating himself he simply turned the radio off and removed the keys from the ignition. Once the music stopped Shell did too throwing up her hood right on cue as if she was prepared for that very moment. Even Pookie had to laugh, "Man bring yo ass on."

Chapter Twelve

At first glance, nothing had seemed to change as far as KeKe's parents were concerned. Shoot, anybody entering the room would assume KeKe was in the same condition she had been in all this time. Disappointment was beginning to take over Shell's face and Pookie looked at her as if he wanted to say, "I told you". Instead, he said nothing and embraced his wife. The moment he wrapped his arms around Shell's small framed body the toughness, the excitement, and all of her strength went straight out the window. She instantly melted in her husband's arms and began sobbing frantically. The sudden heaviness of her body was more than Pookie expected causing him to fall to the floor just as quick as his wife did. Had it not been for the prosthetic leg, he probably wouldn't have been able to withstand the weight of his wife as she sank down towards the floor completely unable to find strength in her own legs to stand.

"I knew we shouldn't have come up here man," Pookie announced as he struggled to get up from the floor.

Shell sat silently and continued sobbing growing more and more irate as time went on. Pookie, the nurse, and a couple walking past KeKe's room had all wanted desperately to interject and say some comforting words to Shell to at least try and calm her down but past experiences reminded them of the importance of keeping their mouth's closed.

Moments later while still occupying a space on the floor, Shell was greeted by the familiar voices of Dr. Tsani and Charmaine. Charmaine had immediately run to Shell's side in an attempt to comfort and console her to the best of her ability. Surprisingly to everyone else in the room, it worked. Shell didn't put up an ounce of fight or rejection. She simply returned the embrace allowing it to ease the pain she was feeling and ultimately bringing her back to sanity.

"Hello, Mr. and Mrs. Flowers," Dr. Tsani stated with a warm smile and an extended hand for a firm handshake.

"How are you doing sir?" Pookie replied while extending his hand, welcoming the handshake. Shell on the other hand said nothing. She tried but couldn't find the words or the strength to have this disappointing conversation again.

"Mrs. Flowers," Dr. Tsani repeated calmly while nodding his head. "Are you okay? Today is a good day, you should be smiling."

"Smiling? What makes you think that? Days aren't so good when you're standing on my side of the fence. Maybe on your side, but I bet you wouldn't want to change places with me to find out." Shell stared into the eyes of Dr. Tsani and waited for a response.

"Well Mrs. Flowers, here's why. As of yesterday Keshawn's vitals have stabilized, she's displayed movement, and we believe she is going to be okay. Of course, we are going to keep a close eye on her and run a few test, but for the most part, she seems to have made a miraculous change for the best."

Pookie clapped his hands together one good time, "Alright!"

Both Charmaine and Shell began going ballistic. While Charmaine got her praise on shouting and thanking God, Shell busted the crip walk again just as she had earlier chanting, "Yeah! Yeah! Yeah!"

Dr. Tsani couldn't believe his eyes. He had never seen anything like this before, but smiled at the obvious excitement and relief the family displayed. While all of this was unraveling, KeKe began to moan.

"Ummm Ummm. Mai..... Mai."

Shell ran to her bedside and grabbed her hand. "It's me baby, how are you feeling?"

"Where is Mai?"

"Mai is okay. She's at home with your sister."

"Excuse me. Sorry to have to interrupt, but I need to do a brief check-up on her

just to make sure everything is normal." Dr. Tsani pulled his stethoscope from around his neck placing the plugs into his ears and tapping on the circular end. "How are you feeling Ms. Flower," he asked while lifting her gown.

KeKe just shook her head as if to say, "Okay".

"Can you take a deep breath for me?" he asked while placing the stethoscope against her chest. "Again." he demanded. "Again." He now placed the stethoscope against her back and demanded, "Now, one more time. And, that's it. Everything sounds good, let me check here," he said slightly lifting her head and gently feeling her lower jaw area, neck, and throat to see if her glands were swollen and they weren't. "Are you experiencing any dizziness or pain?"

"No."

"Do me a favor and look directly at this light. Okay, I'll be back to check on you again shortly."

Once the doctor left the room the celebration continued. The three of them took turns talking to KeKe and asking her questions. Not too many though. They wanted her to save her strength. Besides, they knew what she had been through for the past year now it was time to get her caught up on what she missed. Between the laughs and random smiles that KeKe displayed there also came a little sadness. KeKe realized just how much of her daughter's life she missed. Mai had always been her everything and she prided herself on playing an active role in her life not just sometimes, but all of the time. Then joy filled her soul, as the two most important people in the world to her came walking through the door holding hands.

"Mommie!" Mai yelled after seeing her mother was awake. She screamed so loud that it alarmed some of the others occupying the hospital. Little did they know, it was screams of excitement and many more would be heard throughout the day.

Loc's heart melted at the sight of KeKe sitting in that bed fully alert and free from all of the tubes that had become part of her everyday uniform for the past year. "What up killa!" he said to KeKe knowing it would get a huge smile out of her. KeKe lifted her head and smiled at him. "What are you doing here?"

"What!" Loc spat while smacking his lips. "I've been here every day. You better ask somebody."

"Every day huh?"

"Yup. What you don't believe me? Watch this Cuz, you got me fucked up." Loc left the room for a brief second and returned with Dr. Tsani. "Aye doc, tell her how often I've been up here."

"Well to be honest with you, Mr. Jackson has been here pretty much every day. He's become part of the family here." Dr. Tsani confirmed Loc's statement and smiled giving Loc a pat on the back before he left the room.

"Now what! Yeah!"

KeKe began to cry, allowing her head to fall into the palms of her hands.

"What's wrong baby?" Loc asked as he approached her and wrapped his arms around her.

"I knew you would come, but every day? I love you and thank you so much for being here for me."

"Aww Cuz, cut that out. You're my sis. How am I not gone be here?"

"I know but a year is a long time. Most people would have given up and I'm just overjoyed by the fact that y'all never gave up on me."

This part of the conversation could have went in a totally different direction had Loc not been as humble as he was. Technically speaking, everyone had given up on her. Everyone except for Loc. None of that was important though. Loc was satisfied with the fact that she was alive and able to spend another day with him and his niece. Loc tried hard but was unable to prevent the tear from rolling down the left side of his face. KeKe lifted her hand to his face and gently wiped away his tear. "I love you Loc."

"I love you too my nigga." Loc stared dead into her eyes and allowed his eyes to tell the story his heart wanted to but his mouth couldn't. The love he had for KeKe was like no other and judging by the look in KeKe's eyes, she felt the same way about him. Just as things began to heat up, hearts fluttering, a sudden lump in the throat and a sense of mushiness, Mai ran to her mother's bedside and leaped on the bed landing smack dead in between the two. Had it not been for her innocent, but unfortunate interruption the two of them just might have found themselves in the midst of a passionate tongue twirling match.

Charmaine looked at them, smiled, and shook her head. Her thoughts went back to the time she told KeKe, 'That boy really loves you.' She always knew this day would come. Even in her days of addiction, she saw the love KeKe and Loc shared for one another crystal clear.

"So Mommie, do you love Uncle Loc like a boyfriend?" Mai asked while sitting beside her mother on the bed.

KeKe was caught completely off guard and couldn't speak without stuttering, "Wha-Wha-What? Why would you ask me a question like that?" Her hand was placed gently over her chest as if she was trying to prevent her heart from jumping out of her chest.

"I saw how y'all were looking at each other. Then you was like, 'I love you Loc,' all soft like how the girls do in the movies." Mai spoke softly imitating the girls from the movies and mocking her mother.

Everyone in the room couldn't help but fall out laughing. Even KeKe had to laugh. "No, Mai I don't. And that's not something you need to be worrying your little self about. Where do you get this stuff from anyway? You kids are a mess."

"Mom," Mai spat looking at her mom with her head slightly tilted to the side and her hands on her hips, "I am not a little girl. I'm a young lady and we know things like this."

"Well you know what, 'young lady'; excuse the hell out of me."

"Uncle Loc," Mai turned to him looking for some honesty, "Do you love my Mommie like a girlfriend because she won't answer me."

Loc looked at KeKe and raised his eyebrows in shock. He never answered Mai but made a statement to KeKe. "What? She gets it from you!"

Before the conversation could go any further visitors began swarming in the room saving the day. Mai was kind of disappointed but left it alone. She knew she would get her answer one day; one day real soon. The emotions in that room varied so much that even a counselor would have experienced an emotional rollercoaster.

As the room became more and more crowded, KeKe smiled and thanked God for all the people He had placed in her life. This day would mark the one day she felt loved by many. Her whole life she felt alone and felt as if the people that truly loved her could be counted on one hand. Today was confirmation that that was untrue and would be embedded in her memory for the rest of her life.

The food service worker walked in wearing pink and grey scrubs, carrying a tray that contained a small bowl of soup, a garden salad, and thinly sliced boneless chicken breasts. Once the tray was placed on the table, KeKe thanked the worker and she departed the room, continuing on with her rounds.

"Look who's up and looking better than ever," Kai announced as she walked in the room unprepared for the welcome she received.

Aside from KeKe, the room fell silent and the awkward looks were more than enough to confirm that something was terribly wrong.

"Kai! Oh my god, when did you get home? Come here," KeKe shouted out of pure excitement with her arms spread wide open welcoming her embrace.

Kai made her way toward KeKe reciprocating the same gesture but not before Harmony made a dash for it.

"Auntie!"

"Whoa whoa wait," a few of their loved ones yelled but it was already too late. Harmony bumped the table really hard and knocked the still smoking soup onto KeKe's legs. While everyone else freaked out KeKe laid there like nothing was wrong.

"Harmony!" Kai yelled. "What is wrong with you? Be careful."

Everyone in the room began to panic, some holding their hands over their mouths in shock, some covering their eyes, and others simultaneously saying, "Oh shit."

Loc looked at KeKe and realized she hadn't made a sound. As hot as that soup was she acted as if she didn't feel a thing. "Wait a minute. You didn't feel that?" he whispered to KeKe as he stood beside her.

"Feel what?" KeKe responded completely unaware of what he was referring to.

He looked toward the end of the bed and KeKe followed suit. She knew that Harmony had knocked the food over, but she never realized that there was soup all over her legs. Loc grew suspicious and decided to confirm what he was thinking at the moment.

"Do you feel this?" he asked while poking KeKe in the leg with a toothpick he had in his pocket. KeKe sat waiting on something to happen. She thought that maybe he was playing or something but little did she know her lack of reaction to the poking had cause Loc to drive the toothpick into her leg with more force. So much force that the toothpick broke in half. "Somebody go grab the doctor," Loc requested.

No one moved at first hand, but Charmaine noticed the look on Loc's face and walked briskly toward the nurses' station requesting that they page Dr. Tsani. It only took Dr. Tsani about five minutes to respond to the page and he and Charmaine re-entered the room.

"What's seems to be the problem?" Dr. Tsani asked, directing his question to Loc. Obviously Charmaine informed him that Loc was requesting his assistance in the room.

"Something ain't right," Loc informed him. "Soup spilled directly on her legs and she didn't feel it. I even poked her a few times as hard as I could and she didn't feel that either."

Dr. Tsani looked surprised and pulled an instrument from his pocket and began tapping and poking KeKe in the legs. Loc was right, KeKe didn't feel a thing. Dr. Tsani grew concerned and wanted to try a couple more things before he made a final diagnosis. "Can you all please wait out in the waiting room? The nurse will inform you when it's okay to come back in." Everyone looked at him wondering what was going on. They had been so loud and so distracted that half of them hadn't even noticed there was a problem. "It'll only take a second," Dr. Tsani assured them. Finally, they began to move, making their way to the waiting room as directed. The room was cleared out within seconds; all except for Loc of course. He wasn't going anywhere and Dr. Tsani wasn't going to make him.

"What's wrong?" KeKe asked growing a bit concerned as she watched Loc and Dr. Tsani's reactions.

Loc stood next to her holding her hand and hoping his homegirl wasn't about to have to go through anything else. "You're good baby, don't trip."

"Ms. Flower, I'm going to conduct a brief exam and see if we can figure out what the problem is."

Clearly she had full use of her neck because she was able to look all around the room. Her arms were fine as well, confirmed by her ability to stretch her arms out and grab hold of whatever it was she wanted. Dr. Tsani pressed gently on her abdomen and KeKe confirmed she could feel that. The same went for her back and waistline. However, when he began examining her hip and thigh region, she had little to no feeling at all. A nerve test confirmed that KeKe was indeed paralyzed from the waist down.

"I'm sorry to have to tell you this but; it seems you have a slight case of paralysis."

Since she did have a little feeling in some cases the doctor was sure that she would get better with time. "I'm going to recommend you see a physical therapist at least four times a week. With a little therapy you'll make a full recovery. It may be a long road," he warned her, "but if you stick with it and remain consistent you'll see the results very soon."

KeKe couldn't believe her ears. Paralyzed? This was not happening to her. Had this been a year ago she would have gone ballistic. But after waking up from a situation where she could have been dead, she now looked at life in a totally different light. Sure, her feelings were hurt and she wanted to be able to live a normal life but the way she looked at it, it was better to be alive and paralyzed than dead and unable to see her daughter grow into a woman.

Loc was disappointed as well. As soon as the doctor made his findings, Loc dropped his head low and mouthed, "Damn!" His heart broke every time he witnessed KeKe go through trials and tribulations. Not because she wasn't supposed to, but because it was always the worst trials and tribulations one could ever expect to go through. Ever since he could remember KeKe's had to endure the unthinkable. And all the while, she bore a smile and still looked out for those that needed her. Family, friends, and even those not so deserving of her love had gotten it. But no one ever returned it. But this was it. This vicious cycle was going to end right here, right now.

A tear rolled down KeKe's face and just as he had done on a previous occasion, Loc gently wiped her tear away. Dr. Tsani, saw the hurt in both of their eyes and decided to give them some privacy.

Chapter Thirteen

"Did y'all see how that bitch just walked in there like every thang is cool? I swear I wanted to floor her snitch ass, soon as I seen her raggedy ass."

"Hold up! Don't let no false shit come running out of your mouth. We ain't seen no paper work so until then shut the fuck up. That snitch shit ain't no game and you don't want to be the one putting that type of jacket on somebody and it ain't true. Especially when they got kids," Big Choc jumped on her little homegirl's head. She wasn't trying to hear none of what she was talking about right now.

Kai stood only a few feet away from the girl making the statement and decided to just let it go. Her skin was boiling from the inside out but she refused to bite into the bullshit. The more she stood quiet the more people began to run their mouths.

"Naw Choc fucks that! Hanging at the police station is all the confirmation I need. She's lucky I got love for her sister the way I do."

"Exactly," someone else chimed in.

It was at this point that Kai said forget it. Regardless of what these hoes may think or what she may or may not have done, Kai was far from a punk. She went against everything she knew to be right at that moment and took flight on the ring leader. Kai delivered a whirlwind of punches on her supposed to be homegirl and no matter how hard she tried to throw one back, Kai would knock that shit right down and catch her with another one. Clearly she was no match for Kai so her girl Chest decided to jump in. No sooner than she had, Shawna walked through the waiting room door and dropped Chest right where she stood.

Big Choc walked over toward the door, "Hold up!"

She moved towards Shawna as if she was going to bring harm to her and it proved to be a big mistake.

"Don't do it Choc! On my mama Cuz you don't want it with me," Shawna said matter-of-factly while looking Choc dead in her eyes.

"Ha!" Big Choc laughed as if Shawna was a joke. "Little girl you better sit yo ass down somewhere."

Everyone in the room fell silent waiting to see this outcome. Big Choc was what they call an O.G. and was big as hell while Shawna on the other hand was the next generation and about twice as small in size. On the outside looking in you would fear for Shawna's safety. The thing about this though, was Shawna had been around Big Choc all her life and knew her almost better than she knew herself. To Shawna, Big Choc was far from what others thought her to be and had no fear in her heart at all when it came down to it.

Big Choc reached out to grab Shawna, simply to go somewhere and talk. What happened next would change everyone's perspective of who was who and what was what. Not only that, but it would kick off one of the most controversial hood meetings in the history of the Foe Trey Gangstas.

BOOP, BOP, BOP, BOOM!

Shawna gave it to Big Choc just as she said she would and didn't stop until the big homies grabbed her up off of her. The people in attendance couldn't believe their eyes. Especially the O.G. homeboys. One thing that has never happened and never been tolerated was a young homie disrespecting or pushing up on an O.G. That was grounds for an automatic mad circle, as they called it. A mad circle was when everyone surrounded you and literally beat your ass to a pulp. In this case, it was definitely going to happen.

"What the hell is wrong with you?"

"Fuck that bitch! She always running her mouth and trying to press up on muthafuckas younger than her. These sorry ass bitches," Shawna pointed indicating she was referring to a specific group of girls, "do what she say cause they scary as a muthafucka. I'm not that bitch and never will be. You come looking for something over here, you can bet yo bottom dollar you gone find it." Shawna was mad as hell and letting it all show.

Once she was turned up, there was no turning her down and everyone in attendance knew it.

Big Choc stood behind a crowd of homies acting as if she was mad and ready to demolish Shawna's ass. In truth, she was more embarrassed than anything. Out of all her years of pushing her weight around no one had ever challenged her. Now that someone had, she feared her image was damaged forever.

"You lucky I didn't wanna hurt yo little ass," Big Choc blurted trying to gain at least a couple of the brownie points she had lost.

Shawna didn't utter a word. She just looked at Choc welcoming her to come and run up on another ass whooping if she wanted to.

"Naw, hold up Choc. Let me holler at her for a minute." Ridah grabbed a hold of Shawna's arm pulling her towards the hallway, "Come here man."

ðãð

In the hallway Ridah called himself calming Shawna down and trying to find out what was really going on. He had known Shawna for most of her life and she had never overstepped her boundaries like that. I mean, he knew that she and KeKe had little to no respect for a lot of O.G.'s in the hood, but the way she handled this wasn't normal.

"What happened, Shawna? You know what the business is homegirl so I need to know what the hell you were thinking about when you did that shit." Ridah stood directly in front of her with his arms folded giving her complete eye contact.

Normally she wouldn't waste her time explaining herself to nobody. Since this was Ridah asking the questions she went with it. Especially since he was one of the few she did have the upmost respect for.

"Look, I walk in and see my cousin getting rushed, it is what it is. Then out of all people, Big Choc gone step to me like I'm one of these little buster ass bitches. I'm not having that. I respect her get down because if people gone let you do the shit that she do then they deserve it. But, don't bring that tough shit my way because I'm not them, period."

"I feel you but you know you ain't supposed to be taking off on no O.G. Now you got to deal with what comes next."

"Do I look worried? All they gone do is jump me. Anybody can win doing some punk shit like that but I bet you don't none of them wanna see me head up," Shawna said seriously.

"How you expecting a head up after doing something like that?"

"I'm not expecting anything. I'm just saying, I would respect a bitch that whoop my ass in a head up fade. That jumping shit ain't gone do nothing but make me take it personal and catch all they asses one by one walking through the hood. Then y'all gone be screaming 'Shawna's trippin'.'"

Ridah couldn't help but laugh. He shook his head thinking to himself, "That's them muthafuckin Flowers for you," referring to KeKe's family. One thing they wasn't, were some punks and followers. Shell taught their asses right. "Well it is what it is. Make sure you handle your business."

"Oh, you ain't gotta tell me. You know what it is."

ðð̃ð̃

Back in the waiting room, everyone was conversing about the incident that had just occurred. Even those that knew they should have kept their mouths closed were talking.

"Girl, did you see that? Oh my god that mess was crazy," one of the girls whispered to a friend sitting next to her.

"It's about to go down in the hood. I'm gone make sure I'm there to have front row seats."

"Me and you both," she said still whispering, trying not to make it obvious that she was still talking about that embarrassing moment. For a moment she had gotten nervous. Big Choc walked towards her and stopped directly in front of her. *OMG did she hear me*, the girl thought to herself, afraid of what Big Choc might do to her.

However, Big Choc was only interested in one thing: Gilbert Lindsey Park. "All y'all   come to the park a.s.a.p.," Big Choc firmly stated before walking out of the door.

Everyone knew what she meant and what this meeting would be in regards to. While some shook their heads in disappointment, others were pumped up about the fortunate mishap. For years, some of them craved the opportunity to be able to get with the Flower family, but knew from other occurrences that it meant serious trouble. Not only were they fighters, but some cold gunners and once you fucked with one you might as well be prepared to fuck with them all. This mad circle was the perfect opportunity for them to show how they felt, but, the real question was, is it worth it?

Over half the waiting room left to join the others at the park while some stayed behind to visit KeKe. At least that's what the plan was, up until Dr. Tsani walked in with a few security officers demanding that everyone exit the hospital. "Damn! I wanted to see my girl. You mean to tell me you're not gonna let any of us visit her?" NeNe asked disappointed.

"Unfortunately you all have to leave. With the approval of her brother we have stopped all visiting for Ms. Flower permanently. Any questions, concerns, or suggestions should be directed to the family." Before NeNe could say another word Dr. Tsani concluded, "Thank you for your cooperation."

NeNe's feelings were extremely hurt. Instead of arguing back and forth she accepted the fact that her homies had fucked things up for everyone again. When she made that left turn out the door and down the hallway, Loc got a glimpse of her with her head hung low and called her name, "NeNe!"

NeNe turned around and responded, "What's up Loc!"

Loc jogged toward her with a soda in his hand. "What's up my nigga? I didn't know you were out here."

"Yeah, and them fools did it again! Messing with their ignorant asses, I can't even see my homegirl." NeNe's sadness was written all over her face. She hated the way people acted in the hood. Not only was it uncalled for but it always had an effect on the hood as a whole and they were all either too damn slow to realize it, or too damn selfish to care.

"Don't trip you can come in there with me," Loc suggested while putting his arm around her neck.

"Are you sure? I don't want them to start tripping."

"Come on man, am I sure? I call the shots up in here," Loc announced with an expression of seriousness on his face.

NeNe laughed, "You always think you got it like that. You're not the man Loc! How many times do I have to tell you that?"

"You're gonna be telling me that until you croak over and die because I will never believe that. Shit, you don't believe that yourself. You know I'm the man," Loc stopped in mid stride and did a penitentiary pose; chest sticking out, hands balled up against his chest, one leg slightly twisted with his foot pointed out, and his head held high as if he were the king of the world.

NeNe laughed harder than ever and pushed Loc out of her way. "Boy move your crazy ass out of my way."

Loc laughed just as hard as NeNe did with his tongue pressed up against his teeth. He knew how to make NeNe feel better and it worked every time.

ð..ðð

When they entered the room, both KeKe and NeNe screamed softly with excitement. They were both so happy to see each other. Although they exchanged some genuine smiles, hugs, and excitement, NeNe could sense that something was wrong. She had watched KeKe grow up and knew when something was bothering her.

"What's going on soldier?"

112

"Nothing much," KeKe spoke softly with a smile still spread across her face. "How is my big bro?"

"He's fine. He's been worried sick about you. When I told him the good news he sent me up here to verify it first. He said if they were lying, somebody was gonna get their ass kicked."

KeKe laughed at the thought of Sniper saying those exact words. "Sounds like Sniper to me. I can't wait to see him. How has everything been going with you?"

"Everything is cool with me. You know me, as long as my man is okay I'm okay. When this shit happened to you, our lives were literally flipped upside down. That man loves your ass so much that he flipped back into the old Sniper. I hadn't seen that side of him in so long that it frightened me."

"Oh, you don't even gotta tell me no more. I already know. I'm cool now though so tell him he can calm down."

"I'm gonna let you tell him yourself," NeNe said after dialing Snipers cellphone number.

"Hello," Sniper spoke into the phone.

"Babe, somebody wants to talk to you."

"Who?"

Rather than answer his question, NeNe passed KeKe the phone. "What's up bro?"

Sniper sat silently on the phone unable to say a word.

"Hello."

Still he said nothing. Sniper was speechless and could do nothing but drop down to his knees on the floor of his living room. As tears rolled down his face he thought of the days that has gone by that he had to endure the pain of losing his little homegirl. His heart was pumping overtime as the excitement built up in his brain and brought about a smile.

"Hell-ooooooooo," KeKe sang into the phone one last time.

"What's up KeKe? Cuz......," Sniper began talking nonstop into the phone and assured KeKe that he would be up there to see her personally. He was so excited, he paced back and forth unable to control the movement of his legs. His walk resembled that of a smoker on a mission to find some of that good stuff. KeKe was happy to hear from him and enjoyed his conversation. The excitement he displayed over the phone was enough to wipe away the sadness that KeKe was previously feeling before NeNe and Loc had re-entered the room.

"Well, I'll see you when you get up here. I'm going to pass NeNe back the phone. I love you."

"I love you too. See you in a minute."

"Alright babe. I'll talk to you later," NeNe said immediately after putting the phone to her ear. "Well alright y'all. I'm gonna gone and get up out of here. I have to make it up here to this park before somebody kills somebody."

"Say no more," Loc spat trying to quickly terminate that conversation before it could even begin. The last thing he needed was for KeKe to be worried about some bullshit when she had enough to deal with.

"But, I was about to ask her something. Who's doing what at the park? I hope it ain't got to do with my squad," KeKe said as serious as a heart attack.

NeNe noticed the look on Loc's face and knew not to answer her question honestly. "I don't know but I'm about to go see."

"Alright, well be careful," KeKe stated.

After sharing a warm loving hug with one another, NeNe made her exit and thanked God as she walked down that long white hallway, for sparing her friends life.

It Goes Down At The Park...

Chapter Fourteen

Car after car pulled up into the parking lot waiting to see some action. Kids covered the playground completely unaware of the drama they were about to witness. One by one they took turns sliding down the slide, swinging back and forth on the swings, and running throughout the sandbox playing tag. Laughter filled the air as all of their innocence was displayed, painting a perfect picture of what fun and happiness should be.

Within minutes the parking lot was completely full. Cars were double parked blocking in people they knew and some they didn't. Blue rags painted the parking lot as well as girls of various ages prepared themselves for the ritual commonly displayed when you went against the grain. Since this was female business the homeboys that did attend stood at a distance and enjoyed a drink or two. Their purpose of being there was simply to make sure things didn't get out of hand and to watch the streets for enemies while the homegirls did their thing. Should anybody decide to come through, it was gonna be like the fourth of July around this joint.

Once everyone was in attendance the girls rallied up and headed towards the center of the park where there was nothing but green grass, space and opportunity. To their surprise, when they reached their battle ground, Kai and Shawna were already waiting posted up against the bench. As the girls approached, both Kai and Shawna stood up from the bench and stood face-to-face with their so called homegirls, but soon to be attackers. Judging by the size of the crowd, Shawna guessed it must have been at least sixteen to twenty of them. It was no doubt they were gonna lose this fight but just as Shell had taught them, it was all or nothing. The two of them were gonna stick together no matter what.

During the conversation they were having before the girls joined them, they had already come up with a strategy to survive this battle for as long as they possibly could. Each one of them picked two of the biggest in the crowd and vowed to do all they could to take them down first.

Before anyone knew it, there was a complete circle around the two of them. Big Choc, however, wasn't in attendance.

"Kai, what you looking for? This ain't got nothing to do with you. Your ass whooping is coming on a whole 'nother day. You better hope you even get to fight with yo snitch ass. Right now, we gone deal with Shawna."

Kai was heated but still said nothing in return to any of them. That statement alone was enough to let Kai know that even after this fight she was definitely gonna kill somebody. Rather than respond to what the girl had to say, Kai walked in closer to where Shawna stood. The girls must have taken that as a

117

welcome to bring it on. Within seconds the girls moved in for the kill. Just as they agreed, Shawna and Kai put their backs together and went for what they knew. Blows of all kind were being thrown; jabs, uppercuts, open hand slaps, you name it they did it. Even the weakest links had the nerve to try to get off. For a moment both Kai and Shawna was doing a good job at holding their ground. They were still standing, at least two of the big bitches had already hit the ground, and so far neither one of them was running out of gas as they called it.

The homeboys stood by watching and slapping hands. Although they knew this was something that had to happen, they also knew that this wasn't going the way everybody thought it was gonna go.

"Damn!" one of them said as he shook the homie hand. "Did you see that shit?"

"That's them Flower bitches," he replied with a big Kool-Aid smile on his face. "Those bitches are crazy."

No sooner than he said that, Kai hit the pavement. This was exactly what the other girls had been waiting on. Since Kai was suspected of snitching there were no rules to the way she was dealt with. With this in mind, they began kicking and punching on her like she was the worst of their enemies. Shawna refused to let it be like that. Since they wanted to be dirty she got dirty. She kept on swinging but made it her business to stomp the shit out of any and everybody that hit the ground. That is, until she hit the ground herself.

The kids were now screaming at the top of their lungs. All of their fun had turned into a bad dream. Their parents were working hard to calm them down, but were forced to keep them in this violent environment since they were blocked in. Seeing that this was getting out of control, the homeboys proceeded to break the fight up.

"Hold up! Hold up!" Moe said while pushing the girls apart. With the help of about six other homies, they had managed to separate the wild group of girls. Never in a million years did they think it would be so hard to do. They were sweating and tired their damn selves just from the break up.

"God dammit! Move the fuck back," Moe yelled just about ready to slap a bitch.

Now that the fight was over, the girls picked up their rags, fixed their hair, and began talking shit as if it wasn't over. Kai and Shawna made sure each other was cool and walked toward the parking lot promising to keep their promise and catch these bitches in the streets. As they walked past a big green trash barrel, Shawna retrieved the gun she had stashed before the rest of the girls had gotten there. It was the same stash spot she used whenever she came to the park. Since the police were always tripping, she had to make sure she never had it on her.

Once she had it and put it within her waistline, her and Kai walked briskly to the parking lot bypassing all of their attackers. With the girls behind them, things began to get heated, again. The same girl that talked all the shit at beginning of their meeting started up again.

"Ole snitch ass bitch!" she yelled full of aggression followed through with a glass Corona bottle to the back of the head.

119

"Oh shit!" Kai yelled while grabbing her head.

Once Shawna realized what just happened, she turned around and immediately started busting.

BOOM! BOOM! BOOM! BOOM!

Four shots were fired and three people lie wounded on the pavement.

"Shit! I knew this was gone happen," Ridah announced to the other guys standing around.

Not too many of them were surprised either. The history of the Flowers' told the outcome of this little gathering before it even happened. So while some screamed and hollered unable to believe what was happening, the majority of the bystanders just looked and shook their heads.

Big Choc emerged from a car in the parking lot and released a couple of rounds at Shawna. To no one's surprise but hers, Shawna only got more pissed and returned fire walking directly towards her.

BOOM! BOOM! BOOM! BOOM!

She didn't duck, twitch, scream or nothing; just fired off as many bullets as she had left in her weapon.

It amazed people how bold and unmoved Shawna was during the vicious attack Big Choc had exhibited. But Shawna had blanked out. All she knew was she was angry as hell and somebody had to die. With nothing other than murder on her mind, Kai jumped in her car and headed towards the house. Little did she know, Big Choc was hit and in route to the hospital in a car full of homegirls. In the car were also a few automatic weapons. Had they not had to get Big Choc to the hospital, they would have popped off on Kai and Shawna's ass. Lo-and-behold, the two cars came door-to-door with one another at a light just a few blocks away from the park.

"There she go right there!" one of the girls yelled pointing to Shawna sitting to the right of them.

"Get off on her ass," another girl yelled.

And that's what they did. As soon as they came to a complete stop they opened fire on Shawna's car. Bullets penetrated the car, bursting out all the windows on the left side of the car, and piercing through the metal. Shawna lay in the seat with her arms protecting her head. Not only from the bullets but the glass that continuously flew all over the car. Unable to get a clear view of the road in front of her Shawna crashed into a light pole that sat just off the corner. When the shots seemed to have slowed down, Shawna rose up drawing her weapon to fire the last round she had. One of the girls in the car with Big Choc clearly wasn't built for this type of shit because the moment she saw the glare from Shawna's gun, she got so nervous, she accidently fired her gun. When the gun went off, she pissed on herself. She didn't know if she was shot or what, but was clearly scared as hell. She knew what Shawna was all about and seeing that gun come pointing out of that window caused her to see her life flash before her eyes.

"Ahhhh! Ahhhh! Oh my god! Shit!" one of the girls screamed frantically.

Queen B. G.

No one knew what the hell her problem was. They looked around wondering if she was high and tripping or something. "What the hell are you screaming for Cuz? Calm your ass down."

"Big Choc is hit man, look!" Her hands were full of blood as she tried to stop the blood that was oozing from the back of Big Choc's head. Everyone in the car panicked and began yelling like their lives depended on it.

"Oh my god! What the fuck just happened?" the driver yelled while twisting her body to face the girls in the backseat.

No one understood how this was happening right now. As crazy as it may seem, no one ever even questioned whether or not this was caused by someone in the car. Seeing the gun stretched out of Shawna's window caused them to believe that she fired a lucky shot and met her mark. "Pull off! Pull off! We have to get her to the hospital. Hurry up!" But, Big Choc sat lifelessly in the front seat. Nothing that they attempted to do at this point would have changed the outcome of this awful situation. Her head had already grown limp, while her eyes were still open gazing back at whomever and whatever stood in front of her. Police sirens could be heard in the distance while onlookers watched in disbelief. Cameras and cellphones were being used to record this tragic event. Little did everyone taping know, these devices would soon be confiscated and unreturned, which would also be of benefit to the police once the investigation underwent.

"Come on man, we gotta get outta here. I'm not trying to be nowhere near no dead body when the police arrive."

"We can't just leave her right here like that. She's still our big homegirl."

"You're absolutely right," another girl chimed in.

"What the hell you mean she's absolutely right? If you believe that you are gonna sit here with a dead body and the police not about to take yo ass to jail then you are dumber than a box of rocks. I'm getting the fuck up outta here."

With that said, she went racing down the street with no real destination in mind. Meanwhile, the other girls sat shaken up and torn between leaving their big homegirl and saving their own asses. Even the girl with the gun was still sitting there distraught. She rocked her legs from side to side, pulling at her ears, and wishing that she could wake up from this bad dream. Unfortunately for her, it was real as a heart attack and in about ten seconds she was about to be surrounded by black and white squad cars, uniformed police, and .9mm weapons pointed at her face.

"Run!" someone yelled.

And right on cue the girls all ran simultaneously through the streets trying to avoid the police. Even this part would be visible on someone's cell. Squad cars quickly pulled up coming to a screeching halt. Some officers jumped out and took off after the girls who were now just a short distance away from the crime scene. Others assessed the car and its surroundings trying to make sure the coast was clear. With guns drawn and ready to fire, a team of officers moved in slowly toward the two vehicles. Although quite a few girls had already made a run for it, they could never be certain that there was no one left that would pose a threat to them or their colleagues.

Now in close view of the vehicle, the officers were able to see that someone was in fact in the car. "Passenger, put your hands up where we can see them now!" an officer yelled over the speaker. The long time hatred he had built up towards the gang members of this particular neighborhood had him ready to kill somebody. His trigger finger was itching and all he was looking for was a reason. "Come on motherfucker, move," he said to himself in a whisper while pointing his weapon at his suspect.

However, Big Choc didn't move. The officer repeated his demand once more, "Passenger, put your hands up where we can see them now!"

Still there was no movement. Without her making any type of movement the officers had no choice but to move in for the kill, but not before warning the suspect of their intentions.

"Put your hands up now! If you do not comply with our orders any sudden movement could result in our officers using excessive force." The officers moved in, and were now inside of the car.

"We have a fatality over here," the female officer announced to the rest of the squad while checking for Big Choc's pulse.

"This car is clear!" another officer yelled while putting her weapon back into her holster. Right then, a call was made notifying dispatch about the fatality and homicide detectives were on their way.

ð...ð

With squad cars everywhere; blocking every street in a one mile radius, intersections shut down, the helicopters up and the dogs out, it was only a matter of time before they caught their suspects. Whoever hadn't made it out of this perimeter by now was going down like Tookie Williams. People of all walks of life began to surface on the corners and in their yards observing this tragic event. The officers gave constant reminders of how serious this was and demanded that they go back into their homes so they can secure the perimeter. Some complied while others completely ignored their command and stuck around to see if someone they knew was hurt.

"That's Big Choc!" a local smoker yelled after getting a closer view of the person in the car.

Officers scrambled to try and get him away before he caused a scene. "Sir, can you please go back across the yellow tape," the young officer asked while slightly pushing the man in the direction he wanted him to go.

"Hold on! You don't have to put your goddamn hands on me. That's my people over there," he said still turning his head to look at the damage someone had just caused. "Choc! Choc!" he yelled hoping to get a response from her.

Officer Collins, who stood just a few feet away, overheard the man screaming the victim's name and couldn't believe his ears. He moved swiftly towards the car and made a positive I.D. of the victim. Officer Collins had worked the gang unit for over seven years and was very familiar with Big Choc. The problem with that was he was also familiar with the love and respect Big Choc had in the neighborhood. Her death was definitely gonna spark one of the biggest gang wars Los Angeles had ever seen.

"Sarg, we have a problem," Officer Collins began to explain.

This was definitely something they had to gain control of and fast. Once the rest of the neighborhood got wind of her death it was gonna be catastrophe and nobody knew this better than Officer Collins. Before he could finish explaining his prediction of what was to come, a crowd of people ran quickly to the scene acting in an aggressive manner. Though some appeared to be sweating and out of breath there was no stopping them from getting confirmation on what they had heard.

"I'm gonna need you all to stay back behind the yellow tape please," an officer said while shaking with fear of being attacked by the hostile crowd.

"I wanna see if that's my homegirl over there," Moe stated while lifting the tape attempting to walk right pass the officers to get to Big Choc.

"Sir you can't….," Officer Lions tried grabbing Moe to stop him in his tracks but was unsuccessful. His lack of ability to stop him also caused him to stop in mid-sentence to restrain him before he was able to reach Choc's side. Unfortunately for the police that never happened.

Moe got a glimpse of Choc sitting limp in the passenger seat of the car and sounded off, "It's Choc Cuz! Choc! Choc! Get up homegirl," he yelled loudly while grabbing Choc's arm from the driver's side of the car. Police officers swarmed the car and asked that he back away from the car and stand on the other side of the tape.

"Choc! Choc!" he sobbed.

He fell to his knees and allowed his head to drop onto the seat of the car. Still holding Choc's hand he released a stream of tears begging God to give him his homegirl back. Officers grabbed him by the arms and attempted to raise him from the ground. Big mistake. The whole crowd went crazy causing officers to gather up with weapons drawn demanding everyone leaves the area.

Ambulance from the crime scene within the park proceeded towards the second crime scene with sirens on. The sirens caused a brief distraction with the officers causing them to turn around only to be greeted with an even bigger problem. Gang members from the first crime scene were now approaching the officers from behind. In a matter of seconds the gang members would have the officers surrounded and out-numbered; two to one.

Officer Lions jumped on his radio requesting immediate back up to 43rd and San Pedro. Before he could complete his call, all hell broke loose. Women were screaming and hollering while men shook their heads in disbelief, falling up against cars with their heads resting in the palms of their hands. The more aggressive ones of the crowd threw punches at no one and nothing in particular trying desperately to release the pain and anger they felt at the moment. Just when things were expected to go haywire, everything came to a stop. A call came over the radio saying they had a visual on one of the suspects. Officers began running, while patrol cars hit corners so hard you would think they were gonna flip over, and the gang members in attendance were anxious to find out who their so-called suspect was. If they were lucky they would find them first and gun 'em down the same way they did Big Choc.

ð...ðð

"Where are they at?" an impatient young lady from the neighborhood asked herself as she grew frustrated from the futile search for the so-called suspect.

"I don't know but I'm gone find their ass. I promise you that," her girlfriend responded completely unbothered by the lack of ability to find this mysterious person. All she knew was she had to take this anger out on someone and it was definitely gonna be the person responsible for this.

"I hate walking through this nasty ass shit. Why'd we have to come this way anyway?"

The two girls crept into an alley filled with debris just a few blocks from the crime scene in hopes of finding someone hiding there. The foul odor that dawdled lingered in the air was strong enough to knock you out. Even the sleeve of their jackets covering their noses couldn't stop the stench they tried so desperately to avoid. Slumped over from a weakened stomach and eager to leave the alley, the two friends quickly made an attempt to exit the other end of the alley. About halfway through, where another alleyway intersected with this one, a familiar face appeared.

With squinted eyes the more aggressive of the two asked, "What's up? Why you all out of breath my nigga?"

"The police are on me. I can't shake these fools," the girl responded out of breath and totally unaware of the mistake she had just made.

"Hold up! So they lookin' for you?"

"Yeah."

"Aw hell naw! So you downed the homegirl?"

All this time she'd been searching and anxiously seeking out an enemy only to find out that enemy was one of her very own. Now angrier than she was before, Tika pulled out her gun ready to kill her use-to-be homegirl. As bad as she wanted to pull that trigger she couldn't. Dogs were barking, footsteps were getting closer at rapid speeds, and this was gonna be the one time she was gonna have to just let it be. She wanted to kill her bad but her life was more valuable on the streets as opposed to being confined to a jail cell for the rest of her life. Since running was not an option, Tika made the decision to wipe down her gun and toss it into the bushes and continue walking with her friend through the alley until the police insisted they stopped. Tika and her friend grabbed hands and walked down the alley as if they were a couple on the perfect date enjoying a walk with one another.

When the police approached yelling, "Freeze! Police, don't move. Put your hands up." They just knew it was over.

Surprisingly, one of the officers pointed to Tika and said, "Ladies, please exit the alley as quickly as possible," and held his gun directly towards their suspect.

With nowhere to run and absolutely no way to avoid this from happening, the suspect followed the orders of the officers and dropped to her knees. By the time she was face down in the filth and slicks of long-standing urine, Tika and her friend were at the entrance of the alleyway notifying their folks of who the suspect was. Helicopters still hovered in the air, while dogs barked and pulled violently toward their target. Officers covered both ends of the alleyway and occupied rooftops with a clear shot at their suspect if things should get out of hand. Within minutes, they retreated to their cars giving each other high-fives and pats on the back for a job well done, placing their suspect in the back of the vehicle. As they pulled off, headed to the station, local gang members surfaced watching in awe as they confirmed the killer was in fact one of their own.

ððð

At the station, everything went as smooth as silk. When the charges were made clear to the suspect she told the whole story from beginning to end; everything from the hospital to the park, down to the car crash and the murder. They now knew names, which had guns, which did the driving. Things were about to get real in the field and all because everybody that wanna be down ain't really down, especially when it comes to hood business.

Chapter Fifteen

With the streets still poppin' and all of the family drama building more and more each day, Loc feared that KeKe would lose her mind trying to play her position in it all. He did all he could to keep the news of the world away from her and continue to help her focus on her full recovery. Besides, she'd already given and lost so much to the streets. There was no way he was gonna allow her to throw away her second chance at life.

The phone calls coming in to the hospital were limited to Mai, Loc, and Shell. Even Shell was a stretch, but how could you prevent a parent from interacting with their child? Visiting was the same story with the exception of Charmaine. She continued to come to the hospital to offer some prayer and support to both Loc and KeKe. Whatever it was she could do, she did and with no expectations or strings attached.

"Hey KeKe! How are you feeling today," Charmaine asked holding a bouquet of flowers and kissing KeKe on the cheek. The orange, red, white, and greens of the flowers accented the room perfectly. The aroma was soft and sweet like a splash of Sweet Pea from Bath and Body Works.

"Hi Charmaine! Thanks for the flowers. They smell amazing."

"No problem. I just thought you could use a little brightness in the room."

"Well you were right about that."

"So how are you feeling today," Charmaine asked again as she sat in the chair just a few feet away from KeKe's bedside.

"I'm good. A little frustrated from not being able to do what I want, but blessed to say I'm here to see another day."

"Amen to that."

"And then I have this wonderful man over here proving to be a great support system," KeKe said smiling at Loc. He returned the smile and nodded his head in approval of her statement. "He hasn't missed a beat. He does therapy with me and everything."

"I heard that. So you already started therapy?"

"Yeah, today was my first day. I didn't do much since this was my first appointment but it felt good to get out of this bed. Next week they are gonna send me to therapy at Memorial Care Rehabilitation Institute in Long Beach.

"Oh okay. I heard that's a real good facility. If I'm not mistaking it's connected to Long Beach Memorial Hospital, isn't it."

132

"Yup. At least that's what the brochure said that they gave me this morning."

Loc sat in silence, lost in his own thoughts. While the ladies discussed therapy and things of that nature, he was mentally preparing for some long overdue hood business. Now that KeKe was awake and at least halfway back to her old self, Loc could focus on retaliating against the dude that did this to her. He figured since the hood was already in an uproar he might as well go and do a little damage control himself. All throughout this episode with KeKe, he had a young lady from a local college that he messed with following D to learn his every move, locations, and habits. He told her to consider it a paid vacation. When it all started, he had no idea that the young lady would be sharp enough to get close to D, but she did. She started dating one of his immediate family members that she seen him hook up with on a regular basis. This was a plus for Loc because she could now tell all when it was time to.

When Loc left the hospital that evening he kissed KeKe's forehead and told her, "Baby the next couple of days are gonna be a little different from what you're obviously used to."

Confused and curious, KeKe grabbed him by the hand and asked, "What do you mean different?" Concern was written all over her face and through her eyes he could see that along with that concern stood a great deal of fear.

"I have a few runs I have to make so I won't be here as much, but I promise to call and check on you every chance I get," he stated with hopes that she would accept and understand.

"Alright just be careful."

"I will." With that said, Loc walked out of the room and immediately snapped into gangsta mode. From what the young lady had told him, D was preparing to come back to California and would be staying at the Hyatt Hotel near LAX airport. He would only be in town for two days so he had to move and move fast.

"Tika, what's up?" Loc spoke into the phone making way to his vehicle in preparation to gather his thoughts in the privacy of his own home.

"Oh, hey Loc. I'm just about to load these bags in the car and head to the city. I want to make sure I'm there before he arrives so we can go over the details. I should be there about six this evening, so will you pick me up or should I get a rental?"

"I'll pick you up so we can go over the business and you can just use one of my cars while you're out here."

"Okay, well that's what's up. I'll see you in a few hours then."

"Alright, bet."

The call ended and Loc continued his drive home still pondering on his next move. Although he didn't know the full details of D's visit nor his stay, he was certain that this would be the last breath that D would ever take. He vowed that this day would either be the last day on earth for D or himself and there was no way he was gonna allow this bitch nigga to take his life. His adrenaline began building more and more as he thought about that perfect moment. The moment he wished KeKe could witness with her own two eyes.

KeKe was determined to live a different type of life, but one thing that didn't change was her urge to find the dudes that did this to her. Loc witnessed her pray every day for God to grant her the opportunity to come face to face with them just one more time. She promised that the day she could look them in their eyes would be the day she gave up her old lifestyle forever. Unbeknownst to her, that day was near but what stood in the way of it happening was Loc's commitment to helping her pursue a new lifestyle.

ðð

Lowkey pacing back and forth throughout the living room with 2Pac's, *Hail Mary* playing in the background, Loc had come up with the perfect plan to handle this business. He couldn't, however, say when and where it was gonna happen just yet, but he knew exactly how it was gonna happen. Everything down to the tiniest detail was determined. With all these thoughts in mind, Loc walked aggressively down the hallway and into his bedroom where he kept his weapons.

With both hands, he lifted the mattress, damn near tossing it on the floor, exposing a desert eagle, a .44 Mag, a sawed off shotgun, and a Mack 11. Either one of these weapons was guaranteed to get the job done, but Loc was on some real animosity type shit and prepared for overkill. His weapons of choice were both the desert eagle and the .44 Mag. Satisfied with his choice he placed the two on the nightstand just beside the bed, and replaced the mattress just as he found it. Before exiting the room he removed the bottom drawer to his dresser and retrieved two boxes of bullets, a ski mask, and an old rag which he used to wipe down the bullets and his weapon.

After replacing the drawer he returned to the living room, plopped down on the black suede couch and proceeded to wipe everything clean. While he loaded his weapons, ironically, *If I Die Tonight* was seeping through the speakers of the radio saturating the whole atmosphere with that cold-hearted reality of "what if". This only propelled Loc's urge to stand victorious in the end.

Before he knew it, time had flown by. It was now time to head to the airport to meet Tika. With every passing moment, he grew more and more anxious, but tried desperately to maintain his composure. Even on the short drive to the airport he found himself mean mugging and had to quickly pull himself together. It was a problem he'd had all his life. When he was about to snap, it showed all over his face. No matter how hard he tried it was never something he could conceal. KeKe always told him that it would bring him a lot of trouble one day and for some strange reason he was compelled to make that change. Maybe it was because he felt he owed her a chance to see him with better days especially since he was so adamant about her having them.

Sepulveda Boulevard was jammed packed crowded. It seemed as if everybody and their mama's were either coming or going at the airport. It took about twenty minutes to reach the actual airport and another fifteen minutes or so to find Tika. When Loc pulled up to the Southwest Airline terminal he was greeted with that lovely face that captured his attention one hot summer day. He approached the terminal smiling and there she stood rocking some chocolate brown Coogie jeans with a beige off-the-shoulder sweater and some beige stilettoes to match. Her hair fell flawlessly down her back and was complimented by some gold trimmed Gucci glasses that sat on the top of her head.

"Hey boo," she said excited to see Loc as he approached her to help with her bags.

"Hey Ma," he replied with the same excitement, but avoiding the lip-to-lip contact she tried to give.

"Oh like that huh? Let me find out you're out here acting brand new."

"Never that," Loc said while giving off a fake laugh. "Let's just get outta here. This traffic got me irritated as a muthafucka."

Tika knew it was more than the traffic that he was worried about but decided to just leave it alone and get in the car. Immediately after taking off, Loc began asking questions. He started with a few about her trip so that he didn't have to hear no shit, but his one and only concern was D and that's really what he wanted this to be about. Period.

"So how was your trip?"

"It was cool. If it wasn't for the fat, nasty nigga sitting next to me on the plane it would have been great. Do you know his nasty ass was burping and farting damn near the whole way here? I swear I wanted to knock the shit out of him. I couldn't even eat or drink anything because I was afraid I would throw up."

Loc chuckled a little and gave a reply just for the sake of being polite, "That's crazy. Did anybody else say anything to him?"

"Nope. You know how they be, nose turned up and whispering to their friend or whoever and won't say a word to him."

"Yeah that's usually how that goes."

"So what do you have planned for me while I'm out here?" This was exactly what Loc was trying to avoid. He wanted desperately to nip this in the bud, but decided to be nice, "No disrespect but I'm only concerned about one thing right now. You know how I am about my folks. Let me focus on this business and then we will see okay."

On the inside Tika's feelings were really hurt, but she refused to let it show. "Understandable," she said.

She knew from the jump what type of nigga Loc was and would just have to accept it for what it is. They were never supposed to have sex anyway. It was something that just sort of happened one day and she had secretly fallen in love. It was the best sex she had ever had in her life. And with two more encounters to follow, she kinda just expected it to happen whenever they crossed paths.

Loc knew what the business was, but just couldn't bring himself to mess with Tika. It had nothing at all to do with the business he was pursuing; it had everything to do with KeKe. For the first time in all the years that he's known her, his heart is telling him to that she's the one. Now don't get it twisted, he's always felt he needed a girl like her, but never actually thought that it would be her. With everything looking like it's a promising, yet mutual desire, there was no way he was going to jeopardize it. Especially since, she was in a relationship so close to the man he was out to kill.

"Let's get down to business. Tell me what I need to know."

Tika looked at him thinking to herself, "Unbelievable". But just as he asked, she began to tell him all of the details that he needed to know. This girl had really done her homework and came through for him. When it was all over he promised himself that he would bless her financially and hopefully that would be enough.

ðð̃ð̃

Damn, Tika thought to herself. This boy didn't even try to kick it with me. She sat in the Infinity, coasting up the highway towards her girlfriend's house feeling some type of way. Everything in her told her that he was brushing her off, but could she really trip? He was not obligated to do anything considering the fact that she was not his girl, had a dude, and was never given any impression that she would ever be anything more than a friendly fuck.

"I've got to get this dude off of my mind." But how, she wondered to herself. And then it hit her, just find somebody new. She picked up the phone, dialed her girlfriend up, and made it official.

"Hello. Hey boo."

"Hey Tika! Where are you?"

Queen B. G.

"I'll be pulling up in just about twenty minutes or so. You down for a little girl's night tonight?"

"What you have in mind?"

"I don't know. How about we hit Hollywood and see what's cracking out there. You know that's where all the fly dudes are gonna be at."

"Wait a minute Tika. Since when you want to go looking for some fly dudes? The last I heard you had a good man and the perfect side piece."

"Well that side piece ain't a side piece anymore. He's nothing more than a friend of mines."

"Tika, shut the hell up. You know you are lying through your teeth. Just a week ago you were all on my phone gone over this dude and couldn't wait to see him. What happened to that?"

"Girl, you're trippin'. I ain't never been gone over him."

"Look, there you go lying again," her friend laughed, "Girl get off of my phone."

"I'm serious. So you down or what?"

"Yeah I'm game. But don't flip the script and get to talking all of that lubby-dubby shit. If you do, I'm gone leave yo ass at the club."

"Oh that's what you're not gonna do. I'm driving boo-boo."

"You got a rental?"

"Something like that," Tika said not wanting to add fuel to the fire.

"Something like that? Either it is or it isn't. So...."

"I'll see you when I get there," Tika responded before hanging up the phone. She was avoiding that conversation at all cost because it would only prove her girlfriend right.

Within minutes after hanging up the phone, Tika arrived at her girlfriend's house. She parked the car a couple of houses down so it wouldn't be the first thing her friend would see and made way up the walkway to knock on the door. When the door opened, the two girls stood face-to-face screaming and hugging like little kids. They hadn't seen each other in months and were excited to be in one another's presence.

"Tika!" her girlfriend yelled.

"Hey boo! I'm glad you made it. Come on in and make yourself comfortable."

Stepping in the house was like stepping into an MTV Cribs episode. From the outside you would never know this house could look like this. It had granite tile floors, white carpet, plush-leather furniture, flat screen TV's, a fireplace, and a fish tank in the wall. That was only in the living room and family room. Tika could only imagine how the rest of the house looked.

"Girl this house is nice. You're over here living the good life. Everybody ain't able," Tika said shaking her head.

"It's cool. Since I don't have no man to spoil me, I spoil myself. I'm glad you like it though. I try."

"Try? If this is trying girl I don't know what I've been doing."

Her girlfriend laughed, "You are a mess. It ain't easy and it takes time, I can tell you that. This ain't anything I did overnight. While y'all are out buying clothes and taking trips, I'm spending my money on my castle. If home is right I don't need anything else."

"I heard that. Well I need vacations and stuff. That's just something I can't live without."

"To each their own. Enough about that though. Let me show you where to put your bags and then we can get started on your so-called friend."

"Here you go. Why can't we just put the bags up and get ready to hit the club? Let's get a couple of drinks or something."

"Yeah, that's exactly what I thought. You can get ready in this bathroom right here and I'll use the other one."

"Cool. Just one more question."

"What's that?"

"How much to rent this room? This is something I can live with right here."

"Girrrrrlllll!" she left the room throwing her hands up at Tika as she walked down the hallway and up the stairs to get showered.

Chapter Sixteen

For the second time today, Loc had driven down the block of one of D's known associates. This time was no different than the last. Not one pedestrian in site, a dog, or anything. It struck Loc as kind of odd, but he figured maybe this was a peaceful area in the neighborhood. Not too likely, but not impossible either. He decided to go around the block one more time and sit near the corner where he could get a clear view of the address that Tika gave him. Once around that block and parked on the corner, Loc shut off the lights and the car and waited.

He sat there for minutes watching the house and thinking of tomorrow's course of events. It would be much more hectic than today, but would all pay off in the end. "What the..." His phone began to vibrate displaying the number from the hospital where KeKe was. He started not to answer but was afraid that something could be wrong.

"Hello."

"Hello. What you doin?" It was KeKe.

"Nothin', what's up?"

"Just checking on you. Is everything cool?"

"Yeah, everything's straight. Is everything alright with you?"

"Yup." KeKe said hiding the fact that she missed him like crazy today.

"Okay, well I will talk to you in the morning then."

"Alright."

With that, Loc hung up the phone and KeKe didn't feel right about it. She could tell something was up, but didn't quite know what it was. What she did know was she was gonna let him do his thing and say a long prayer for him before she closed her eyes tonight.

ð ð ð

There it was, the navy blue Dodge Durango that Tika told him to look out for. It pulled up directly in front of the address she'd given and sat there with the music playing loud enough to hear at the other end of the block. No one entered or exited the car, just sat there as if their plan was to kick it. Loc didn't mind. When it came to the business he would wait for days, weeks, and years to capture his target and put 'em to rest. Just as the music played in the truck, Loc enjoyed the music that played in his car. The first thirty minutes of waiting went kind of cool. Now that they were nearing hour number two Loc was growing frustrated and getting a little antsy. His entire bag of weed was gone, the cd had played all the way through twice already, and these muthafuckas were still sitting in the truck. Loc had decided he needed to stretch his legs a little bit, but didn't want to leave and take the chance of losing them. Against his better judgment, Loc emerged from the car looking as edible and fly as he wanted to be.

"Aye homie," a voice just a few feet away stated capturing Loc's undivided attention.

"Who you talking to?" Loc asked to clarify that it was him the guy was talking to. And it was.

"Where you from big dawg?"

Loc couldn't believe his ears or the young punk's audacity to even ask him a question like that.

"Check this out young homie. I didn't come over her for all that. I came to see my folks and that's it that's all. I really ain't got time for no bullshit."

"Fuck all that! I asked you where you from," the dude said bluntly looking Loc straight in the face as he talked.

Loc looked at the little dude in disbelief and began approaching him from the driver's side of the car. Surprisingly, he didn't budge just stood there completely unaware of the beast that he had just awakened in Loc. As soon as he was within arm's reach, Loc grabbed him up by the collar of his shirt, twirled him around, put him in a cold choke hold, and stated his claim. "Don't you ever get at a real nigga like that. That's exactly how you lose your life." With that said Loc snapped his neck and allowed his body to fall limp on the pavement. Luckily for him, no one had seen the incident occur. Looking around at all of the nearby houses Loc noticed a bunch of untrimmed bushes and dragged the little dude into the bushes. Once there, he ensured that the dude was completely covered and returned to his car to complete his stake out. Just as he thought, they had already exited the car. The good thing was he knew which house they entered in. The bad thing was he still had no idea what the hell the dude looked like or how many people were with him in the house. With that in mind, Loc decided to abort this plan for the night and try again tomorrow.

Chapter Seventeen

"Tika, I better see some action when we get in here, too. You thought you were slick playing that music all loud and stuff so we couldn't talk on the way here, but you're not. I'm not gone say nothing though. If you wanna lie to yourself then that's your business. I know the real, though and as soon as you try to call me with that lubby-dubby shit, I'm gone make it my business to deliver a nice pop in yo mouth."

"OMG! Are we really gonna do this?"

"Nope. We are going up in here to find us some keepers." Her voice was full of sarcasm and Tika couldn't say a thing.

"Whatever."

The club was poppin'. The DJ had everybody on the floor doing their thing. The house was packed to the point that you could barely maneuver through the place, but once you hit that dance floor you were good. The dance floor at Boulevard 3 was huge. The special guest for the night was Trey Songs and judging by the way the women in here were dressed, he was definitely gonna do some choosing tonight. Even the big girls were representing. And don't get it twisted, there were some that were fly enough to be on the front cover of a magazine. Who said you couldn't be big and beautiful?

When Tika hit the dance floor, all eyes were on her. She danced like a girl straight out of a Uncle Luke video. Ass was everywhere wobbling like a big bowl of Jell-O and by the looks of it, it took no effort at all. She barely moved but her booty was having a seizure. When she dropped it to the floor the crowd went wild. Her girlfriend stood close by and watched as all of the men drooled over her friend. Her face displayed a smile that said, "Yeah boo, you did that", and then the two slapped each other a high five.

"Bitch, you did that. You ain't gone find no keeper showing them all of your tricks like that, but hey, at least we know you definitely found another side piece."

The men approached the ladies back-to-back trying to get Tika's number in hopes of hitting that while finding out what other tricks she had up her sleeve privately.

"Girl that's all I need," Tika responded before eyeing the guy she absolutely had to meet. When he noticed her connection with him, he pushed past the rest of the dudes and sat beside her at the table. As awkward as it may seem, the thirsty dudes behind him continued in their pursuit to get her attention. Epic fail! The dude sitting next to her had her undivided attention.

"Hi. My name is Bam, what's yours?"

"Tika."

"Nice to meet you Tika. Can I get you a drink or anything?"

"Sure. I would like a Tequila Sunrise please. Thanks for asking."

"And what about your friend, what is she having?"

"Oh, you can get me the same thing, thanks," she said budding into their conversation to speak for herself.

Bam began to laugh at her boldness and said, "Cool. I'll be right back."

"Tika, you know you are a mess right."

"Girl why, what did I do now?"

"You did not have to go out there and show your ass like that. You big show off."

"I know right. But I know you ain't mad 'cause you know how to get off too."

"Oh, I ain't never mad. I don't want none of these thirsty ass niggas anyway."

"Mo' power to you. I do!" Tika spat loudly completely unaware that Bam was standing by her side listening. "I thought you were gone to get us some drinks."

"I was, but I ran across a waitress and put in the order so that I don't have to wait in that line. Is that okay with you? I can leave for a little while longer if you'd like."

"No it's cool. It was just a question."

149

"Okay. So where is your man at? I know a beautiful young lady like you has one."

Tika's girlfriend couldn't wait to hear the answer to this one. She put her hand up against her face and leaned a little closer over the table looking at Tika through curious eyes. Tika caught a glimpse of her silly self and just shook her head at her and responded, "Naw, I just have friends."

With that said Tika's girlfriend almost choked off of her drink. Bam looked at her asking, "Are you okay?" But she couldn't respond. Her eyes were watery as she patted her chest to try and clear her throat from coughing.

"Don't pay any attention to her. She's always a bit extra," Tika alleged as she looked at her girlfriend like she had had enough.

"I'm gonna let you two love birds get better acquainted, I'm about to hit this dance floor and have me some fun."

"Yeah you do that," Tika responded sarcastically while giving off a phony grin. With her gone Tika and Bam engaged in a pleasant conversation about nothing in particular and shared a few laughs in the process. Although the conversation went good in the beginning Tika found herself getting bored quickly and desperately wanted her friend to come back to the table. *Damn I hate when fine ass dudes ain't got no conversation for me, it just messes up everything*, Tika thought to herself. No sooner than the thought crossed her mind Bam opened his mouth to ask the question he'd really wanted to ask all along.

"So you going home with me tonight?" Just as bold and serious as a heart attack.

Tika looked at him and laughed, "You don't even know me and you wanna take me home, what kinda shit is that?"

Bam looked at her surprised, "Oh like that? You sure was wobbling that ass like you was ready to give it up. Don't walk the walk if you ain't ready for what comes with it." Just like that, the conversation was over. Bam had stated his claim and was ready to shake the spot. But Tika wasn't finished just yet. There was no way he was gonna make her feel like a piece of shit and just walk away like it didn't just happen.

"Don't get mad at me because I can do what yo bitch can't and have absolutely no intentions on letting your raggedy ass hit this!" Although he was walking away, Tika was determined to have the last word and was sure to project her voice more and more the further away he had gotten.

Bam didn't even acknowledge her words, just kept on walking as if she was the nothing ass bitch he made her out to be before he walked away from the table. Had it not been for the fact that his girl came to this club, he would have turned around and knocked the shit out of her, but he wasn't about to put his business out there like that and risk his girl finding out. A conversation was nothing. She knew he had female friends. But a fight, oh she would have killed him on sight.

Still upset and ready to flip out, Tika sat at the table guzzling down what was left of her drink. Her eyes wandered around the club scanning the crowd for her friend and she was nowhere in sight. Once her drink was gone, she maneuvered through the crowd to the dance floor and found her girlfriend getting it in with a fly ass Jamaican dude. They were winding and grinding like it was nobody's business. Their bodies were in sync with one another adding an even sexier feel to the song that played through the sound system.

When the song was over the two of them shared a hug and smiled at one another. As she walked off to join Tika, who stood just a few feet away, the guy eased up behind her and whispered something in her ear. Tika wished like hell she knew what he said because whatever it was had her girlfriend smiling from ear to ear like the Kool-Aid woman.

"What you smiling so hard for?" Tika asked eager to find out what he said.

"Girl, nothing."

"Oh like that huh?"

"Girl why are you in my business? Where is Mr. Man-of-the-Hour?"

"First off, you are my business. Second, he pissed me off."

She laughed, " Are you surprised? He only hollered at you because he wanted some of that ass."

"I can say the same about the dude that just had you grinning like the fucking Joker."

"No boo-boo you can't. We didn't exchange numbers, nor did I put on a strip tease for his ass to make him want me. We danced. You know, what grown-ups do when we come to the club, and left it at that."

"Alright Ms. Sarcasm with your smart ass mouth. If that wasn't a strip tease then what was it? All you had left to do was take your clothes off."

"You are a real hater Tika. That's how you dance to their music."

"Whatever. Let's just leave."

"Ohhhhhh, so you ready to go now because you mad? I thought we came to find a fly dude for you. I see a lot of them in here and you ready to leave because of one?"

"Don't start." Tika grabbed her by the arm and started towards the exit.

Her girlfriend didn't say a word, just went with her. But as soon as they made it outside where there was no loud music she gave her a low blow, "And don't get in the car talking about your side piece because I don't wanna hear it."

Tika felt bad because that's exactly what she planned on doing. *So much for that idea*, Tika thought to herself. I'll just call him when we get back to the house. Forget her.

Chapter Eighteen

About an hour before the sun came up, Loc walked into the bathroom and took a shower. The water was enough to wake him up out of the drowsiness he'd felt just moments ago. After stepping out of the shower and wrapping a towel around his waist, he stood at the sink wiping away the steam from the mirrors to reveal his muscular physique and his pearly white teeth. While brushing, he admired himself and was pleased with what he saw. Everything down to his rippled six pack was pure perfection.

Time to do this shit, he thought to himself after using the towel to wipe the excess water that dripped from his mouth after rinsing. His uniform for this cold, foggy morning was the same as usual: all black everything, with a blue rag to compliment it. He grabbed a banana from the kitchen on his way out and it was on. Destination number one, the address Tika had given him to holler at the dude in the Dodge Durango.

As he pulled up on the block he realized his timing couldn't have been better. Two guys, looking just as dumb as a box of rocks were exiting the house and headed down the walkway toward the truck. There was no time to park the car and come back on foot as Loc planned to so he slowed down and waited for them to reach the sidewalk just before the curbside where the truck was parked. Still having perfect timing, he pulled up on the two dudes and put on his square voice.

"Um excuse me! Can you tell me which way the 10 freeway is from here?"

These dudes had to be half asleep or something because even a child knows not to walk up to a stranger's car but they did so anyway. As they approached the car, Loc raised the blue rag over his face, just above his nose and rolled the window down. When they reached the car in an attempt to give him the information, six shots were fired hitting both of them in the face multiple times. Just as quick as their bodies had hit the pavement Loc was hitting the corner headed to dump the car and jump into something else. Destination number two was next on the list immediately after doing so.

ð ð ð

"Aye big homie, what's up?" Loc said to his Mexican partna as he walked up to shake his hand.

"What's up Loco? I'm over here just chillin' fool."

"Well I got something for you." Loc slid him a wad of cash while exchanging the handshake.

"What you need?"

"Burn this muthafucka up!"

"You got it big homie."

"A'ight, I'll get at you later. I got some shit I gotta do."

"Bet."

Just like that everything was handled. Loc and everyone in his circle knew to keep business real short and sweet. He left out of the garage and walked around the corner to Moe's house and jumped in his other car. He parked it there for days like this. Still in his mode and sticking to the script, he drove towards destination number two and prepared for war. If what he was told was true it was go hard or go home and nothing but death was gone stop him from going hard in the paint.

ððð

Showtime, Loc thought to himself as he began loading up for the war that had been declared at destination number two. Dressed in all black once again with the same blue rag hanging from his neck, Loc hopped into the stolen vehicle he had and headed out. No matter how hard he tried to remain focused on the situation at hand, his mind continued to wander back to KeKe. He wondered if she was ok, if she was upset or just giving him his space, and if he should tell her what he was up to.

Fifteen minutes into the drive, Loc hit the number to the hospital, which he had on speed dial, and spoke to KeKe for what could be the last time. He tried hard to conceal the anger and frustration he possessed, but KeKe could see right through it.

"Hey KeKe. How you feelin?"

"I'm good. How are you?"

"I'm straight. You know the Loc is always straight."

"Where are you?"

"I'm in traffic right now. I got a little business to handle and then I'm gonna come see you."

"Loc," KeKe said with a voice full of concern.

"Yeah?"

"What's going on? And don't you dare lie to me."

Loc was speechless. If he answered her question she would get upset and be stressed out to the max. If he didn't she would go crazy and start to question the closeness of their friendship. With that in mind Loc decided he would just give a half-assed answer. "Nothin you need to worry yourself about and definitely nothing I can't handle."

"Loc don't do that. Be real with me. I knew the day you walked out of here that something wasn't right, but I let you do you. For days you've been gone and completely disconnected from me, and I never said a word. Loc we've been around each other for years. I know you better than you know yourself. I mean, I understand you may not want me to get all worked up and that's fine, but how in the hell do you sit here and lie to me like I'm a nobody ass bitch?" KeKe was tired of his games and the bullshit stories he continued to whip up. Today was the day that he was either gonna come clean about his so-called business or watch her erupt like a volcano.

"KeKe don't go there. You know what it is Cuz. I'm out here doin' the same shit I been doin, nothing more nothing less.

157

I don't know what you want me to say. You were right here with me doing this shit, so I'm puzzled as to what you are really asking me."

"Don't bullshit me Loc. You know exactly what I'm asking you. There is something in particular that you are focused on right now and none of it feels right to me. If I didn't give a fuck, I wouldn't ask you any questions, but since I do, I'm expecting you to answer me."

"Look KeKe, there's nothing for you to be worried about. I'm cool baby," Loc stated hoping that his calm and subtle tone of voice would ease the conversation a bit and bring KeKe back to that peaceful place she's dwelled in over the past couple of weeks.

"Loc," KeKe screamed out of frustration knowing full well he was pulling her chain.

"Baby, I promise! It's nothing you need to be worried about."

While Loc and KeKe argued back and forth, Loc was pulling up to destination number two. He knew this was the wrong time to try and end this conversation, but if he didn't it could cost him his life. Instead of the sad story of how he really had to go, he decided that now was a better time than any to exchange some heartfelt words with KeKe.

"Baby, I promise you that if anything was wrong I would tell you, okay. I know who's with me out here and I would never take that for granted. After today, everything will slow down. I'll be there by your side first thing in the morning."

KeKe smiled from the inside out and melted at the sound of those words. "Okay."

"I love you."

"I love you too."

"Get you some rest."

"I will."

"Movin'."

"Bye."

"No! Bye could mean forever. Say you'll see me later or something."

KeKe smiled once again and said, "Movin."

Charmaine sat close by, smiling as if she could hear their whole conversation. She was admiring the infatuation the two shared. Right before her eyes their love grew stronger and stronger, becoming so evident that it was impossible to hide.

"KeKe, why do the two of you have to be so hard towards one another? Y'all so crazy; y'all say 'Movin' when y'all should be saying "I love you". Is that so hard to do?"

"No Charmaine, it's not hard at all. And since you must know, we did exchange those words. I could repeat them all day but, this is all so sudden and I don't want to allow the 'I love you's to run him off. You know men are scared shitless by those words."

Charmaine laughed, "You're right about that. But Loc is his own man and the two of you share something special. That type of love is only found once in a lifetime. You better do what you have to do to keep it before it passes you by."

KeKe looked at Charmaine and took in everything she said. Charmaine was absolutely right but how was she gonna capture the moment without pushing him away? KeKe thought long and hard about her next move and quickly decided it was all or nothing. The first chance she got, she was gonna lay it all out on the table and pray to God that she didn't regret it.

Seeing the sudden change in KeKe's facial expression confirmed for Charmaine that KeKe was definitely gonna take her advice. Eager to get the ball rolling she decided to help her out a little bit.

"Now KeKe, when he comes, you make sure you ease him into the conversation. Don't just blurt it out because then he's gonna think you are crazy as hell, which you are, but, that's not important right now. What you should do, oooh, tell him the good news about how you were able to take a couple of steps today in your therapy session." Charmaine went on and on rambling faster than a southern mechanic taking a cigarette break.

"Whoa! Whoa! Slow down Charmaine. Breathe! You are more excited than I am. I got this though. I'm just gonna let it out and however it comes out is how it's gonna be. What's the worst that can happen?"

Neither one of them really wanted to know the answer to that question, but it was something they certainly needed to think about. No sooner than the thought had crossed her mind she called Loc back. Unfortunately, she got his voicemail so her urge to release all of the feelings she'd been holding in would have to wait until he showed his face at the hospital the next morning.

ðððð

Hours had gone past as Loc sat patiently observing his surroundings and taking a mental note of the faces he'd seen enter and exit the house he planned to exterminate. Loc counted at least six people that sat scattered all throughout the living room. Parked a few houses from his destination on a street that was pitched black thanks to the street lights being out, Loc said a silent prayer and exited the stolen vehicle with a fully loaded weapon in each hand and one in his waistline. The bandana that covered the lower portion of his face was the only thing slightly visible as he maneuvered closer toward the location Tika reported as the house D would be staying in. Loc approached the house with caution and came to a standstill once he was situated at the living room window on the left side of the house. The poorly groomed bushes aided him in remaining undetectable.

As he looked through the window to get an idea of how many people were inside the house and their location, he was shocked to see Kai sitting on the far side of the living room watching television. *What the fuck is she doing here*, Loc wondered to himself. Her presence changed his plans completely. There was absolutely no way he was gonna go in and spray the house with her inside. Regardless of what the streets assumed about her, Kai was still like a sister to him. And with KeKe improving the way she is, he refused to be the reason she relapsed and gotten worse.

His only two options now would be to pick their asses off one by one as they excited the house, or leave and try again another day. Being that he didn't plan on coming into contact with law enforcement, he decided to leave and come back tomorrow. As he turned to walk away from the house a car pulled in to the driveway of the home next door. The bright headlights shinned on Loc causing him to freeze like a deer, wide-eyed and spooked. The neighbors, who occupied the vehicle, caught a glimpse of him as well and screamed to the top of their lungs. Dogs began to bark from the other side of the gate and just as he proceeded to make a run for it, D and his friends emerged from the house with guns drawn eager to find out what all the commotion was about. Luckily for Loc, he was quick on his feet and had enough ammunition to get a nigga up off of him because as soon as they walked off of the porch and onto the grass and sidewalk, they saw him and got it cracking.

Boom! Boom! Boom! Boom!

Gun shots went off almost immediately and lasted for what seemed like an eternity. The neighbors ran and took cover inside their home, while the occupants of D's little getaway home scattered around the yard releasing bullet after bullet in Loc's direction. Loc ran for cover and sat against the side of a ran down Ford pickup truck that sat about a half a block away with his adrenaline pumping at rapid speeds and his trigger fingers itching to show these niggas some real gangsta shit.

The shooting began to slow down quite a bit confirming for Loc that they were almost out of bullets and he was about to make his grand appearance. He peeked around the truck to get a visual of his attackers and almost got his face blown off.

Shhrooon

The sound of a bullet flying right past his ear. It was so close that he could feel the heat of it as it zoomed past and hit the headlight of the car directly behind him. "Aw shit! Cuz!" Loc shouted as he turned quickly and sat his ass down on the pavement with his back against the truck and his hands fiddling with his ear to make sure it was still there. While he did that, one of his attackers was slowly and quietly approaching from the passenger side of the vehicle that shielded him. Loc sat there still in shock from what had just happened totally unaware of the fact that they had gotten close to him.

Boom!

A shot was fired followed by the words, "Ole punk ass nigga," and Loc sat wounded with blood oozing from his left leg. Before the unidentified man could get off another shot Loc had raised both of his weapons, one in each hand, and in the blink of an eye fired about six shots into the body of his attacker. Loc had no idea where the other attackers were but knew that he had to get to his car and fast. With his adrenaline still pumping heavily, he used that extra energy to get up from the ground and make way to his car. Two more dudes were approaching and found themselves almost face-to-face with their Maker.

Boom! Boom! Boom!

The shots kept going. Loc released so many bullets on his attackers that you would have thought you were in the middle of World War V. Sirens could be heard in the distance, alerting Loc that it was definitely time to get away from there, and he did just that. He backed away from his attackers while shooting his way out and jumped into his car. Determined to get as many of them as he could he drove past the house with his window down, arm stretched out and emptied his clip on what was left of the guys defending D. They shot back of course but their weapons were no match for what Loc was packing. The war was just about over and done with, that is until Loc saw with his own two eyes that one of the shooters was Tika.

"Hold up," Loc said out loud. "This bitch got me fucked up." He slammed on the brakes, threw the car in park and jumped out one last time. His aim had always been next to perfect and he used that to his advantage to prove a point at this very moment.

Tika feared what was to come and wished that she had never allowed her feelings for Loc to consume her. She fired at him out of anger, but now that he was up close and personal with her ass, she knew that she had fucked up. As Loc approached her, she tried reasoning with him, "Loc, wait. Let me explain."

"Bitch fuck your life," he spat while releasing three bullets just a few feet from where she stood piercing her right through her forehead and once in her chest.

The last nigga standing made complete eye contact with Loc but was scared shitless and threw his hands up. Loc looked at him and shook his head before pulling the trigger again only to find he was out of bullets. His victim was so afraid of him at this point he didn't even try to shoot back. He simply kept his hands up and watched as Loc got into his vehicle and fled the scene.

When the police finally arrived, bodies laid scattered up and down the block. One down the street by the truck, one in the middle of the street, one in the driveway and Tika on the grass of the home they occupied prior to the shooting. "Are you okay?" an officer asked the young man standing in the grass lost in space.

The young man said nothing. He stood silently looking at Tika's lifeless body which laid at his immediate right and shed tears. His heart was broken and his soul was aching. The reality of her being gone had caused his body to shut down. He couldn't move if he wanted to and grasping the fact that he's allowed it to happen was the hardest thing he'd ever had to do. "Did you know her?" the officer asked as he caught a glimpse of the tears that continued to roll down his witness's face.

The young man shook his head yes.

"Is she your girlfriend?" the officer questioned realizing he wasn't gonna volunteer any information. The young man shook his head no. "A friend?" He shook his head no again.

The officer stood in front of the young man observing him. He also took a look at the deceased and realized they shared some of the same features. His next question would cause a literal break down and confirm why the young man was reacting in the manner that he was. "Is she your sister?" The young man shook his head yes and cried profusely. His legs weakened and he fell to his sister's side and begged her to get up.

"Tika! I'm sorry sis. Get up! Get up sis, please." His choice of words raised a red flag with the officer.

"What are you sorry for?" the officer asked hoping for a lead. But the young man didn't respond. The officer placed his hand on the young man's shoulder and asked again. "Son, what is it that you are sorry for? This isn't your fault."

"I was supposed to protect her. I'm her brother, and I didn't help her," the young man sobbed while still looking at his sister lying on the grass in a pool of blood.

"So you know who did this?" the officer suggested.

Before the young man could respond Kai walked up and answered for him. "Yup. It was that crazy muthafucka Loc. I swear I think he be high or something. I seen the whole thing from the house."

"And you are?" the police officer asked.

"I'm Tika's girlfriend, and I ain't about to let my dog go out like this," she proclaimed.

"Would you be willing to come down to the station and talk to us?"

"Sure will." Kai was high as I don't know what and running her mouth like there was no tomorrow. She was already in a world of trouble over having diarrhea at the mouth but she obviously could care less.

Just as she had agreed to get in the patrol car and head over to the station, Detective Marshall joined them on the grass. "Ms. Flower, what are you doing over here? Don't tell me you know these people."

"Yeah I do."

"How do you know them?"

"I'm friends with Tika," she said pointing to her deceased friend. "And I know…." There was a long pause before she continued her conversation. She had gotten a sudden light go off in her head and she needed to confirm some things before she told them anymore.

"Are you guys gonna pay me for this information, too?"

The officer looked at her and Detective Marshall as if they were crazy and wondered what the hell was going on. Detective Marshall knew that this was about to get ugly so he excused himself along with Kai and headed toward his car with her arm firmly held in his hand.

"What? Why are you pulling me like this? You are hurting me." Kai was unaware that she had fucked up.

"Get in the car. Get in!" Detective Marshall demanded and hopped into the driver seat to speak his piece. "Why would you ask me a question like that in front of another officer? Have you lost your mind? You must be high or something because you know better."

"Sorry," Kai whined. "I just thought since I worked for you now that I would be compensated for any information I give you."

"And you will, but that's nobody else's business. Next time, you wait until we are alone or I'm with my partner and then you talk to me about that. Not in public, not around other officers, and certainly not out loud for the world to hear. You got that?"

"Yes!" Kai said with her arms crossed and an attitude to match.

Detective Marshall emerged from the car, opened the back door, and ordered Kai to leave. Now he had to figure out how he was gonna explain this to his fellow officer.

Chapter Nineteen

Loc stopped at the warehouse to get rid of the car and jumped into one of his own. After racing down the highway through some crazy traffic on the freeway he finally reached NeNe's house. Just as they always did, he parked in the garage and entered through the side door. NeNe was waiting with everything she needed handy and got right to work as soon as Loc entered the room.

"Man this shit hurt homie," Loc said to NeNe while she performed the necessary techniques to getting this leg right.

"It's supposed to hurt Loc, it's a bullet wound. Why won't you sit your ass down somewhere? You were doing good for a while and now that KeKe is almost back to normal you have just done up and lost your damn mind."

"NeNe don't start. I know what I'm doing okay."

"Yeah, I do too. You're about to lose what friend you have left in that girl. And if that's what you are trying to do then, by all means, keep up the good work."

Loc thought about what NeNe said as she stitched him up and placed clean bandages on the wound. About a month before KeKe had awaken from the coma, Loc found himself wishing that he would have just expressed his true love for KeKe before it was too late. Now that the opportunity was here and NeNe putting it the way she did, he was gonna make sure he handled that today. As soon as he was done with NeNe he was headed straight to the hospital.

ð ð ð

"So how are you feeling now, huh?" Charmaine asked excited about the progress KeKe was making.

"Excited and blessed. To be honest, I was so afraid of being confined to a wheel chair that it wasn't funny. I prayed every night and asked God to just give me the strength to deal with it. All this time that I believed God for an emotional breakthrough he was working on it all and I am so grateful. Just last week it was one step, now today it's four. I'm gonna be walking in no time."

"I know that's right," Charmaine smiled while witnessing the transformation KeKe was going through.

Just as quick as the two of them had found a reason to celebrate they were presented with a reason to go H.A.M. Loc walked in with an unfamiliar limp and a facial expression that told a million words. Charmaine shook her head in disappointment, but kept her opinion to herself. Instead she let KeKe handle it, as she knew she would and sat back in her seat.

"Hey KeKe! How you feeling this morning," Loc asked as if everything was normal.

"Don't 'hey' me. What happened to you?"

"What?"

"What my ass, Loc. What happened to your leg?"

"Awe it's nothing. I'm straight."

"Loc, tell me what the hell is going on," KeKe shouted. "I know you haven't been out there doing no bullshit. I'm sitting in here trying to get my life back on track and you act like you want to see me go backwards because of a nervous breakdown. I don't have time for this shit," KeKe stated but got cut off by Loc.

"KeKe listen…."

"KeKe my ass. If you want to continue living that life Loc then you go ahead. I could've been dead over this shit and not one person would have given a damn. I'm done with that shit and with you. I thought we were on the same page but you clearly don't give a fuck."

Loc heard everything KeKe said, but was determined to be heard himself. "Damn it KeKe just listen. I know how you feel about this shit now, but would I be here if I didn't care?"

"Obviously," KeKe retorted cold heartedly.

"Really? So if that was true will I be doing this," Loc kneeled down on his good knee, pulled a little blue box out of his pocket and popped it open.

171

Queen B. G.

KeKe couldn't believe her eyes as she looked down in front of her at the one man who never let her down and who'd always been by her side. Charmaine rose from her seat with the biggest smile in the world on her face and her hands placed on her hips. "KeKe, I love you more than life itself. I've watched you hustle, I've watched you hurt, and I've watched you take care of everything and everybody around you. Now, it's time that somebody takes care of you. Let me do the hustling, the providing, and the protecting. All I need you do is say yes and let me do the rest." Loc looked into KeKe's eyes as her tears flooded her cheeks and let his eyes confirm for her everything he had just said. Before she could give a reply Loc spoke again. "Say yes babe. WE would love it if you did."

KeKe looked confused and began to sniffle, "We?"

Mai emerged from the hallway looking as cute as pie wearing a denim skirt, white tank top, denim sandals, and a denim High School Musical handbag. "Yup! We want you to say yes Mommie."

KeKe smiled and cried even more at the site of her daughter. With her there and in agreement with the whole thing KeKe couldn't wait to reply, "Yes."

Mai and Charmaine clapped while Loc rose up from the floor and kissed his new fiancé long and passionately while his arms held her close.

"I told you, you loved him like a boyfriend, Mommie," Mai shouted. And everybody burst out in laughter.

When Loc released KeKe from his arms, he placed a huge princess cut diamond ring on her finger worth $30,000. KeKe loved it of course and kissed her man once again.

Charmaine walked over and hugged the new couple and gave them the best of wishes while silently thanking God for blessing the two of them in this way. Their union, in her opinion, was one of the best the streets had brought together. Just as they were inseparable as friends, Charmaine was willing to bet her last dollar they would be just as inseparable as husband and wife.

"Don't think this gets you out of hot water," KeKe informed Loc with tears of joy still flowing freely from her eyes.

Loc smiled at KeKe's usual expression of toughness and replied, "I don't think that at all, baby."

"Liar!"

Loc knew full well that after a stunt like that, KeKe was going to overlook whatever the problem was and bask in this moment of joy. After all that she had been through, he knew there was no way she would allow anything negative to overshadow this incredible moment. "Loc, whatever it is, fix it. If you don't, then all of this was for nothing."

Loc looked her right in the eyes and promised her that he would. "I will babe. Just give me a couple more days and I promise you will never have to worry about these streets again." The look in his eyes told her that he was sincere and just as he knew she would, KeKe accepted the promise he put on the table and focused on their happiness. By the looks of things, Mai was focused on the same thing. Her petite little body lay flopped across Loc's lap, giggling from the way he tickled her both under her arms and under her neck.

"Are you gonna leave me alone? Huh? I can't hear you."

"Yes! Yes!" Mai yelled while laughing and trying her hardest to break away from his hold.

"Alright then."

Once she was released from his hold, Mai ran straight to her mom and gave her a big hug. It was moments like this that gave KeKe the strength to keep living and without bitterness. The ability to see her daughter another day and with a smile on her face was enough for her. At this very moment it was worth more than having the ability to walk again.

When all of this unraveled, KeKe was officially on cloud nine. The moment she had dreamed of all of her life was finally becoming a reality and although she was the happiest she'd been in a long time, nothing could erase the nightmares she continued to have once she was alone in the darkness of her lonely hospital room. Every night KeKe envisioned that horrific moment when her life was almost taken. She remembered their names, remembered their faces, and prayed every night that she got the closure she needed to mentally and emotionally forgive them.

After spending hours of smiles and laughs with the ones she loved, the moment she dreaded had quickly approached. Loc and Mai said their goodbye's along with the exchange of a few kisses and hugs. Charmaine said goodbye as well and promised to see them tomorrow for their usual visit.

"Bye Hun, I'll see you tomorrow. I'm not sure what time I'll be here because I have to meet with these Detectives in the morning. God knows what they want. They've met up with me more times than I can count and not once, have they given me any information that was important. Really, I want to tell them to go to hel,l but then there's this little speck of hope I have dwelling within me. I don't know. Every time they call me I get a little anxious thinking that maybe my baby will get some justice. I know that it's a long shot, but hey, you gotta have hope when you have nothing else, right?"

KeKe just nodded her head and put a smile on her face. She could relate to the words that were coming out of Charmaine's mouth, but didn't want to be fake or phony by saying anything that would imply she was on her team as opposed to being on her own sister's team. Regardless of the situation or the relationship Charmaine and KeKe had established, family still came first with KeKe and nothing would ever change that.

Charmaine sometimes wondered where KeKe stood when it came to her daughter's death. She knew without a doubt that KeKe would always ride for her home team but the question was, was she doing it in this case because she had to or because she truly didn't believe Kai did it? Either way, Charmaine had left it in God's hands and knew that He would deal with the person who murdered her daughter, accordingly.

ð ð ð

"So, you are the bitch that killed my little brother?"

Boom! Boom! Boom!

"Wait!" KeKe jumped up out of her sleep breathing hard and sweating profusely.

What she thought to be blood oozing from her wounded body was nothing more than the perspiration acquired from this horrible nightmare. Now sitting in an upright position on her bed, KeKe used her gown to wipe the sweat from her face.

"Why won't it stop?" she questioned to herself. "Lord, you have to take this away. I can't continue to have nights like this. I'm ready to put all of this behind me. I will give anything to have a normal peaceful life. If you just grant me the ability to sleep peacefully and maybe even see my attackers one last time, face-to-face, then maybe, just maybe, I'll find closure and be able to say goodbye to the lifestyle I once lived. I'm ready Lord, Amen." KeKe said this prayer almost every night and although she meant every word she sometimes wondered if seeing them would bring the closure she was looking for or raise more anger and tension. Either way, it was what she wanted and waited patiently on God to bring it to pass.

A Few Weeks Later...

Chapter Twenty

"So how does it feel to walk in and out of your home on your own?" Loc asked his fiance' as he watched her maneuver through the living room towards the kitchen to put dinner on the table.

"It feels wonderful!" she replied with a smile on her face.

"I can imagine. It feels good to watch you do it."

"If I would have been confined to a wheelchair, would you still want to marry me?"

"Where did that come from? Of course I would. My love doesn't come with limitations."

That statement caused KeKe's heart to light up. If there was ever a question as to why Loc was the one, it was definitely answered in that moment. "That's why I love you. Give me some kisses."

The two shared a passionate kiss standing beside the kitchen table where dinner sat, smelling so good that Mai had come to see what it was.

"Uh, y'all nasty!" Mai said as she walked in on the end of their kiss. "What's for dinner?"

"Who are you calling nasty little lady. It's called love. You will learn about it in a few years. Tonight we are having your favorite."

"Louisiana Chicken," Mai asked with excitement.

"Yup Louisiana. Are you ready to eat?"

"Yes ma'am, let me go wash my hands. Don't let Loc eat the legs because if he do I'm gonna be real mad."

"Well in that case give me two," Loc responded waiting to see how fast Mai would come running back to the table.

Within seconds Mai appeared from the hallway dripping water all over the floor. Both Loc and KeKe burst out in laughter and sat down at the table to eat. Mai immediately joined them and dried her hands with a napkin that sat beside her plate.

Bam! Bam! Bam!

A loud, disturbing knock echoed throughout the house. "Who in the hell is that," Loc questioned as he made his way to the living room. KeKe was not too far behind after signaling for Mai to go into her room. No one knew where KeKe's house was besides her family. She kept it that way for the safety of her daughter. This was a life that she inherited but that vicious cycle stopped with her. There was no way she was gonna expose that life to her daughter and tonight would be no different.

"Who is it?" KeKe yelled with Loc standing at her side waiting for a response.

"Police, open up!"

"Police," KeKe whispered with a confused look on her face. "Go in the room with Mai," she demanded to Loc as she prepared to open the door. Once he was out of view she opened the door and asked, "Yes, how may I help you?"

"Are you Keshawn Flower?"

"Yes."

"Are you here alone?"

"No I am not, my daughter is here. Why, is there something wrong?"

"Well we would like to ask you some questions about DeWayne 'Loc' Jones. Do you mind if we come in and take a look around?"

"Yes I do mind. Do you have a search warrant?"

"No ma'am we don't."

"Okay, well in that case, I suggest you get one. What does looking around my house have to do with him anyway? He doesn't live here."

"Well we have information that suggest otherwise. According to our records, he does live here."

"And what records would that be because clearly they are wrong. Nobody lives here but me and my daughter. That's it that's all."

"Well, do you know where we could find him?"

"Nope, and even if I did I wouldn't tell you. Isn't that called snitching? Snitching gets you killed Officer, and I have no plans on bringing that kind of problem to my household. But you already know that, right?"

The officers stood at the door mad as hell, but determined to keep their cool. They didn't want to scare her to the point where it gave her the impression that Loc needed to run. "Okay, well if you change your mind, give us a call." The officer leaned in a little closer handing KeKe a business card. "And if you happen to see Mr. Jones, have him contact me also."

"Sure," KeKe spat with a fake grin on her face.

When the officers turned to walk away KeKe did as well. Once she closed the door behind her she watched them through the living room window to ensure that they left and called Loc into the living room.

"You can come out babe."

"What the fuck did they want?"

"They wanted to talk to me about you. They said that they had information stating that you lived here. Who could have told them that?"

"Don't look at me shit, I didn't tell nobody nothin'. Don't nobody know where I live so I'm definitely not gonna tell no one where you live."

"Well they got it from somewhere. What would they be looking for you for anyway? You told me you ain't been out here doing nothing."

Mai stood just a few feet away watching her Mom argue with Loc. It hurt her feelings to see them fight because they never did that before. But, at the same time, Mai knew that her Mom wasn't gonna let up. One thing she knew for sure was that her mom had absolutely no tolerance for bullshit - around her daughter and her house at that. This was about to get real ugly and Mai knew it. She decided to take her food in her room and close the door just as she knew her Mom would want her to do.

"Babe, hear me out."

"Hear you out? So you've been lying. Go ahead Loc I'm listening."

"Okay, well first of all when I told you I was through with these streets, I was serious. But, at the same time, I'm not ever gone pass up the opportunity to get the niggas that did this to you. You know that."

"Are you serious? So I'm about to lose you too? I'm tired of this shit!" KeKe was upset. Although she appreciated the fact that someone was willing to ride for her the way she would ride for them, she couldn't accept the fact that the drama was, once again, about to take over her life. *Can I just be happy for once,* KeKe wondered. "We still have to figure out how they knew to come here. Shit, you haven't even moved out of your house yet."

"I bet you it was your snitch ass sister," Loc stated matter-of-factly.

"Hold up," KeKe snapped as she swung her head around to face Loc. "What you will not do is call my sister no muthafuckin' snitch. That's a jacket you won't give her."

"Shit, that's what she is. Don't get mad at me Cuz."

"You know what Loc, just leave it alone because in a few minutes this shit is gonna get out of control and this is exactly the type of mess we are not supposed to go through."

Bam! Bam! Bam! Bam! Bam!

The knock on the door this time was almost identical to the last.

"Who is it," KeKe yelled, still frustrated from the escalating conversation she was having with her fiancé'.

"It's me."

KeKe looked through the window and came eye-to-eye with Charmaine. Against her better judgment, she opened the door and let Charmaine in. She let her in out of respect because she had definitely been a great friend, but Lord knows this wasn't a good time at all.

"Hey Charmaine! Can you come back, maybe tomorrow? Now is not a good time."

"What's going on in here?" she asked looking back and forth at the two of them and entering the house anyway, closing the door behind her.

No one paid attention to the tears that dampened her face. They also failed to acknowledge the pain that pierced through her voice as she spoke.

"We are having a private discussion. Do you mind?"

"Whatever it is, I'm sure you guys can work it out. It can't be that bad, is it?" she asked looking at Loc for a response.

"We talkin' about her snitch ass sister," Loc blurted out without hesitation.

"You know what, oooooooh, Cuz, you got one more time. Just one more time. Call my sister another snitch and it's gonna get real ugly in here. This shit ain't no game."

"You know what,'" Charmaine said, "you are right. She is a snitch though. She told me that you were the one that killed my daughter." With those words, KeKe looked at Charmaine in disbelief. She couldn't believe the words that just flowed freely from her mouth. "How could you KeKe?" Charmaine questioned after taking a gun from her purse and pointing it directly at KeKe. "My baby loved you. I loved you. I've been here taking care of you and...."

Bam!

While looking in the direction of Loc but slowly approaching KeKe, Charmaine was caught with an unexpected blow to the face. Before anyone knew it, KeKe had fired on

Charmaine with a cold right hook that was so powerful it sent her crashing down to the floor and her gun flying across the room. KeKe used this as an opportunity to run into the kitchen to grab her .380 from the kitchen drawer. Due to her limited ability to use her legs she didn't make it there as quickly as she anticipated. Loc intervened and tried to stop Charmaine from getting to her gun, but was a few seconds too late. Before he knew it, *Click-click,* Charmaine had cocked her weapon and was prepared to shoot.

At the same time, ironically, KeKe was now standing a short distance from her own weapon. "Charmaine, listen to me. Do you really believe I would do something like that? Think about it, I did everything to take care of her. I treated her like she was my own." As she tried to plea with Charmaine she tip-toed closer and closer to the drawer.

"You damn right I believe her. What reason does she have to lie?"

Mai walked in from her room completely unaware of the severity of the episode that was occurring. She heard the arguing, but thought that it was merely about the officers that came to the door just a short moment ago. KeKe tried her best to signal her daughter to go back into the room without being detected by Charmaine but to no avail.

Pow!

KeKe grabbed her .380 and returned fire. At least seven shots were fired before it was all said and done. Charmaine lie unconscious on the living room floor from being shot by both Loc and KeKe at the same time. Sadly, just like Charmaine, Mai laid wounded on the kitchen floor from being shot by Charmaine.

"Oh my god! Hold on baby, Mommie is here." KeKe said to her daughter as calmly as she possibly could, considering the circumstances. While holding her baby in her arms, KeKe placed a call to 911.

"Mommie, it hurts," Mai whined, staring at her mother with tears in her eyes.

"I know baby, but you are gonna be okay. I promise. Just relax okay."

"Umm hmm," Mai replied.

"911 what's your emergency?"

"My daughter has been shot! Can you please send an ambulance to….." KeKe gave the dispatcher the address to her home and demanded that they get there fast. She was so concerned about her daughter that she totally forgot to mention that there was another gunshot victim needing their assistance as well.

Loc ran to their side unable to believe what he was witnessing at the moment. He cradled Mai in his arms after taking her away from KeKe and decided he would drive her to the hospital himself. Luckily, KeKe was still thinking with somewhat of a clear head and stopped him in his tracks.

"Babe, you can't take her to no hospital, they are gonna take you to jail. As a matter of fact you don't need to be here either. Go ahead and leave and I'll be sure to call you to let you know what's going on." The anger the two of them displayed prior to this incident had flew out the window. Just as always, they had one another's back.

"Are you sure babe? I don't think leaving y'all is a good idea. I'm supposed to be here for you, especially at a time like this."

"Babe, pleeeease. Do this for me. I would rather you be gone for a moment like this than to be gone forever. You are no good to us in jail, now go." She looked Loc in his eyes and kissed him firmly on the lips.

"You're right. Okay, call me as soon as you know something."

"I will."

"I love you."

"I love you too."

"Mai, be strong baby. I love you and I'll be here soon as you get home okay," he said a tad bit louder than a whisper while kissing her on the forehead.

"Okay. I love you too."

Loc proceeded to leave out of the backdoor and walked along the side of the house towards the front to hop into his car and hit the freeway. Since his home was probably under surveillance he decided to chill out at Moe's house. About an hour of driving and two blunts later, Loc pulls up to the house only to find that Moe was gone. He searched his pockets for his key but couldn't find them. This bothered him because he always had his keys on him. The first thing he thought was, maybe they fell in the car. He searched and searched both the driver's side and passenger side of the car, but found nothing. That's when it hit him. He had left the keys at the house. With now being the worst possible time ever to turn and go back he decided to go to Plan B: Shawna's house. This time he called to verify that she was home.

"Hello."

"Aye Shawna, what's up?"

"Hey Loc, what's up wit' you? What are you doing calling so late, is something wrong?"

"I need to chill at your house for the night. I'll tell you about it once I get there."

"Okay well, I'm not at home right now, but I can be there in like the next fifteen, twenty minutes."

"Cool. I should be pulling up in that same time frame."

"Alright."

"Movin'."

With that, the call was ended and Loc pulled out of the driveway headed back to the freeway again. He hit the 110 freeway and allowed the night's air to fill his car. His mind wandered hoping that Mai was okay and at the same time wishing he would run across Kai's snitch ass so that he could knock the shit out of her. Once he made his exit off of the freeway and headed south down the empty street he found himself trying desperately to calm himself so that he didn't do anything stupid. He had to stay focused and available for KeKe should she need him.

While sitting at a red light, he noticed another car sitting at the same light, opposite side of the street with two dudes in it. He only paid attention to it because of the loud music. When the light turned green they drove past one another and Loc got a good look at the one person that had the power to make him lose control and go crazy out here in these streets, D. And D had gotten a clear view of him as well.

"That's that punk ass nigga right there homie," D said to his friend in the passenger seat of his car.

"Then let's get that fool," his friend replied.

Loc was thinking the same thing, grabbing is gun off of the passenger seat and busting a bitch in the middle of the street.

Pow! Pow! Boom! Blaka!

Gunshots filled the air and sounded like Independence Day. Once it was all said and done D had been shot and crashed into a light pole that occupied the street corner, his friend was unconscious due to the crash, and Loc sat unconscious as well with his head limp up against the door panel. Since it was late at night, no one saw the accident. The three guys sat there with their lives slowly drifting away and not one person around to save them.

By the grace of God, a car slowly approached the scene with the ability to get these people some help, but totally unaware of what lied a few feet ahead of them. The driver of the car looked around and realized that people were still in the cars.

She pulled over and attempted to help. The first car she ran up to had two occupants in it; one whom was still unconscious and another that sat moaning in agony from the injuries caused by both the accident and the gunshots.

"Sir, relax. I am about to call an ambulance right now."

The man just nodded his head okay and rested his head up against the headrest while holding his stomach to try and bare the pain. Before running back to her car she stopped at the other vehicle to check the condition of that person. What she saw when she approached the vehicle would change her attitude completely.

"Loc! Loc, get up," she said as she used one hand to lift his head off of the window of the car and the other to open the door. "Get up my nigga. Come on." *This can't be fuckin' happening right now,* she thought to herself. Still, Loc didn't move. She pulled him out of the car allowing his body to lay on the cold pavement. His gun fell to the pavement as well and sat right beside him. Once on the ground Shawna was able to see that Loc had been shot. The looks of this was enough to convince her that there was a shootout. She immediately went back to the first car and demanded information from the driver of that vehicle.

"What happened? Look at me," she said grabbing his face forcing him to look at her. "What happened?"

The unfamiliar man shook his head as if he didn't know. It was at this moment that Shawna got a good look at him. Her adrenaline pumped wildly causing her to become way more anxious than she needed to be at the moment. "D? Is your name D?"

The guy nodded his head yes and found himself face-to-face with his Maker. His response sent Shawna into a vicious attack. She dropped his head from her hands, grabbed the gun that sat on his dashboard, and slapped the shit out of him with it.

Bam!

"Oh yeah, my girl KeKe sends you her regards," she whispered with her lips inches away from the left side of his face and blew his face off with three shots at point blank range. While placing a call to 911, Shawna took her shirt off and threw it into the trunk of her car, grabbed some hand sanitizer and cleaned the blood that splattered onto her face, arms, and hands, and sat beside Loc's car waiting for the ambulance to arrive. She talked to him for what seemed like forever in hopes that he would find the strength to hold on and he did.

When the police and ambulance arrived, she watched nervously as they placed Loc on a gurney and prepared to transport him to the hospital.

"We are gonna need you to answer a few questions," an officer insisted as he approached her with his little tablet in his hand.

"That's fine."

"Did you see what happened?"

"No. I had just gotten off of the freeway and saw them out here. I pulled over and called you guys for help."

"So you don't know any details about the accident?"

"No sir."

"Was anyone else out her besides you and the victims?"

"Not that I saw. There hadn't been any cars or anything to come through here."

"Okay well, we're just gonna take your name and number in case we need to ask you anything else."

"Okay."

Shawna voluntarily gave them her alias along with a fake phone number and drove off into the night. Her first thought was to call KeKe, but she kept getting her voicemail. She called Charmaine to see if maybe she was at her house but got her voicemail too. *Fuck*, she thought to herself. Now she had to drive over to her house to give her the bad news in person.

ððð

At the hospital KeKe sat in the hallway nervous, awaiting her daughter's return from the operating room. Her renewed relationship with God allowed no room for crazy outbursts. Instead, she prayed her way through the pain. She believed without a doubt that He could and would bring her daughter out of this. In the midst of her prayer a familiar voice caught her attention.

"KeKe! KeKe! Where are you?" It was Kai. Her timing couldn't have been better. KeKe was hungry for some of that ass and with all of this space and opportunity KeKe was gonna get off in that tonight.

"Oh my god, KeKe, how is she?" Kai asked completely unprepared for what was to come as she approached her sister in an attempt to hug her and get more information about her niece.

Bam!

KeKe fired on her ass and kept 'em coming at rapid speed.

"Bitch! Fuck you, you ole snake-ass bitch!" KeKe yelled while pounding on her sister like an enemy in the streets. She never wanted to harm any of her family, but this bitch had done enough. There was no other option left other than this ass whooping and KeKe was determined to make sure it was the best one she'd ever had in her life.

Kai tried hard to defend herself, but was no match for her older sister. Kai had literally touched everything in that hallway; she bounced from wall to wall, off of tables and chairs, and even had a long encounter with the floor topped with a few stamps of hatred from the bottom of KeKe's shoe. Kai couldn't believe the pain her sister was inflicting on her and for no reason at all. At least that's how Kai saw it.

The way KeKe was tagging her ass you would never know she had just been through the problems she'd been experiencing with her body. *Hell*, Kai thought to herself, *if this is how she is injured, I would hate to see her in full capability.*

Hospital staff and security came from various directions attempting to break up the fight. Trying to stop KeKe was like trying to stop an angry bear in the woods. It took a while, but they did it.

"What the hell is wrong with you?" Kai asked with blood seeping out of every visible place on her body. Her face was swollen like the elephant woman and her leg appeared to be broken as she limped down the hallway accompanied by hospital security.

"You know what you did. If you don't then that ass whooping should make you wanna figure it out. You bet not bring yo snake ass around me and mines ever again in your life. That's on my Granny, rest in peace. Every time I see you I'm gone get in that ass. You better be glad I didn't kill you bitch!"

After getting Kai out of KeKe's view and convincing her to calm down, the nurses informed her that her daughter would be out of surgery soon. As if things couldn't get any worst, the emergency room doors opened and paramedics came through with a gunshot victim. As the gurney glided down the hallway and passed KeKe she got a glimpse of the love of her life and almost fainted.

"Wait! What is going on? What happen?" The EMT's as well as hospital staff ignored her like she wasn't even there. She yelled at them hoping for some answers, "That's my husband. Tell me what happen, please!

The nurses took Loc to the back while the EMT's confirmed KeKe's relationship to the victim and informed her of the shooting. She immediately fell to her knees and began to pray in a way she never had before. She gave God all she had and commanded Him to fulfill His promises to her. He promised to never leave her or forsake her, He said that if she called on Him and believed that He could do all things then He would. KeKe bowed before the Lord and cried out "thank you. Over and over again she thanked Him for the miracle He was about to perform in her life. No one bothered to intervene especially since she wasn't doing anything wrong. The onlookers looked at her like she was crazy as hell, but there was one old lady that sat across the room smiling and clapping her hands. The people around her wanted to know what she was so excited for.

"What are you clapping for," a woman asked, "That lady is crazy as hell."

"No she's not," the elderly lady responded. "She knows exactly what she's doing. She needs some things to happen in her life and that's exactly how you get it. Everyone in here can learn something from her."

KeKe arose from the floor and paced back and forth across the room still repeating the words "thank you". And then the police emerged through the doors.

"Keshawn Flower?"

"Yes," KeKe replied with tears in her eyes.

"You are under arrest for the murder of Bianca Taylor. You have the right to remain silent. Anything you say can and will be used against you in the court of law."

As they tried to Mirandize her, KeKe went off. "Hold the fuck up. Get these handcuffs off of me. My daughter and my fiancé is in surgery right now and I'm not going no muthafuckin where until I know for sure that they are okay. If you are gonna take me to jail then fuck it, take me, but you are not taking me out of her before I can make sure my daughter is okay."

"I'm sorry Ms. Flower, but you have to come with us. Your daughter will be well taken care of. Child Protective Services is in there with her right now."

"Child Protective what! I will beat your muthafuckin' you know what. Let me go. Let me out of these goddamn handcuffs now!"

"Ma'am, I can't do that. I need you to calm down though."

"Calm down my ass! Let me out of these cuffs."

KeKe twisted and turned throwing a temper tantrum determined to get to her daughter's bed side. The officer's however, stood firm in what they came to do and totally ignored the show she put on. Kai reappeared from the other end of the hallway with a devious grin on her face. KeKe was going to jail just as she waited for her to do and she didn't feel shit about it. As long as it wasn't her sitting in jail for all of those years Kai could care less. Once upon a time she would have felt bad for what she had done to her sister, but now that she had attacked her and the money was about to come in, oh well. *She wanna be hard all of the time, let her sit her hard ass in the pen and see how hard she is in there*, Kai thought to herself.

Things were going haywire in the hospital on this night and it seemed to only be getting worse. Especially once the officer informed her that her fiancé would also be placed under arrest once he got out of surgery. KeKe realized how useless her tantrums were and dropped to her knees once again praying for

God to step in. She spent at least ten minutes on her knees before the officers rudely interrupted and began escorting her out of the emergency room doors. Right at the doors entrance, the lead detective on Bianca's case came face-to-face with KeKe and his colleagues that performed the arrest.

"Hold on. I have new evidence that proves without a doubt that you are the one that killed Bianca Taylor. You are definitely going to rot in jail." Detective Banks appeared to be talking to KeKe, judging by the way they were standing at the time of his statement. But, to everyone's surprise, he was referring to Kai. He walked right past KeKe and placed Kai under arrest placing his handcuffs tightly on her wrist. "Remove the cuffs off of Ms. Flower please," Detective Banks demanded. The arresting officers looked confused and wondered what was going on. The envelope Detective Banks held in his hand was lifted in the air and slightly shaken while he spoke. "I went over all of these statements carefully and cross referenced them with information we'd gotten from other witnesses. Things just weren't adding up correctly so I took it upon myself to get a search warrant for our suspect's home and found the murder weapon. Ballistics confirmed that the bullet that killed Bianca Taylor was fired from that weapon. We also got information confirming Kai's involvement in the shooting that she informed us was carried out by Mr. Jones."

"So after the surgery and everything, my fiancé is free to go, too?"

"Yes ma'am. I apologize for any inconvenience or embarrassment this may have caused."

KeKe was the one smiling this time as she looked at her raggedy ass sister and said, "Boom! Have fun in that hell hole, boo."

Kai was escorted away and KeKe sat relieved. This was a night that she would never forget in her life, but a testimony that would surely change someone else's life. Hours later she was informed that both her daughter and fiancé were gonna be okay and would be able to go home in a couple of days.

G STREET CHRONICLES PRESENTS

DEALT
Wrong
HAND

A NOVEL BY
QUEEN B.G.

TOP NOTCH PUBLISHING PRESENTS
BRIDGE 2 DESTRUCTION
THE SEQUEL TO
"DEALT THE WRONG HAND".
A NOVEL BY QUEEN B.G.

TOP NOTCH PUBLISHING PRESENTS...
DO NOT EN
Crime Scene Do Not Cross Crime Scene Do
JUSTIFIED
Crime Scene Do Not Cross Crime Scene D
A NOVEL BY
SEQUAIA REED

THE TREACHEROUS TALE
OF EBONY & IVORY

Not MY SISTER'S KEEPER

THE DEBUT NOVEL FROM

Sequaia Reed